YOUR LOVE BELONGS TO ME

DEBORAH WALLACE

Your Love Belongs to ME

Published by Deborah Wallace

Copyright © 2020 by Deborah Wallace

5/22

ISBN 978-1-951457-09-9

Cover Art by Raymond and Deborah Wallace

Chapter 1

Shawn Gordon zoomed along the busy street on his bicycle. He'd barely have time to make it back to the office for his four o'clock appointment with a new client. A gust of wind blew his brown hair into his eyes and he brushed it back. Instead of going to the gym, he should have gotten a haircut.

At the edge of the driving lane, he kept an eye out for passengers in parked cars. A couple of near misses with opening doors had trained him to be cautious.

This time of day, his bike was faster than a car. Ahead, a right turn signal flashed, and he cut to the left to go around the car, knowing the driver wouldn't notice him coming alongside.

Two blocks from the office. Relief. A glance at his watch showed he'd have two minutes to spare. He hugged the curb in a no parking zone. Without pausing, a woman in a navy skirt suit, cell phone to her ear, rushed into the street in front of him.

"Damn!" He swerved, but she moved into his path and he struck her with his shoulder. She spun, and fell to her hands and knees. He skidded to a stop, dropped his bike and turned.

As she sat back, her panicked voice hit him. "My phone! Where's my phone?" She looked around frantically.

Must not be too badly hurt if her phone was more important. Shawn guessed at the trajectory of the phone, and spotted it within inches of a storm drain. He trudged over and picked it up. Cell phones should be issued with a license. The woman could have been hit by a car if he hadn't knocked her down first.

A glance around showed how oblivious everyone around them was. Passers-by continued walking, not noticing or not caring that this woman had been struck down by a cyclist. Everyone had someplace else to be.

A female voice on the phone screamed, "Kayli, Kayli? Are you there?"

He walked back and noted the tremble of her hand as he extended the phone to the woman he assumed was Kayli. Half her hair had fallen from its bun, and she pushed the wavy, brown locks behind her ear. "Thanks."

She stared into traffic as she put the phone to her ear. "Michelle, call an ambulance. I can't lose him. Call me back as soon as you know which hospital they're taking him to."

No wonder she was so distracted. It sounded pretty serious. Whoever this guy was, he was important to her.

Kayli dropped her phone into her lap, and squeezed her eyes tightly shut, tunneled her fingers through her hair, freeing the rest of it. She held her head as if trying to prevent it from exploding. It was then that he caught the sparkle of her rings. She was married.

"We really shouldn't stay in the street like this. Are you hurt? Can I help you up?"

Her head snapped up and her beautiful, dark brown eyes widened. She came up on her scraped knees. That had to hurt against the pavement. The tight skirt didn't allow enough movement to bring her heeled shoe up, so Shawn grabbed her elbow and helped her to her feet. The top of her head just reached his nose. They stepped to the sidewalk and he asked again, "Are you hurt?"

"I don't have time to be hurt."

"Well, in case you end up needing treatment, here's my

card. I did run you over." If she weren't married, he wouldn't have minded a call from her. But, likely he'd never see her again.

She took his card and shoved it into her purse. "I've got to go."

She glanced up and down the street this time, before limping across to a shiny, black Camry and driving off.

"I hope that guy appreciates how much she cares for him. I would." He retrieved his bike from the side of the street. A check of his watch told him he was already late.

~~~

Her fear for her son dominated every thought. Kayli hadn't seen Michael yet and had no idea how bad he was. Michelle said Michael had curled up in a ball and panted, but the children hadn't been playing that hard. When she'd put her hand on his chest, his little heart had beat so fast she couldn't count it. By acting so quickly, Michelle had probably saved her namesake's life. Kayli thought of the note in her purse. It was no accident that brought her son to the hospital.

A gray haired woman, across the room, stared at a television screen in a corner. A couple, sitting several seats away, held hands and whispered. Muted voices over a speaker in the hall reminded her she was at a hospital and not in a doctor's office.

All eyes shot to the short, wiry doctor who stopped in the doorway and scanned the room. Gray speckled his hair and tiny wrinkles radiated from his eyes as he squinted into the room. "Mrs. McAllister?"

She jumped up. "Yes. How is he, Doctor?" She'd been strong during the wait, but now, facing the doctor and the concern in his steel blue eyes, tears threatened to overtake her.

"He should make a full recovery, but we'll keep him overnight for observation."

"But what's wrong with him?" Kayli didn't want to believe someone had tried to harm her son. She held back from grabbing the man's arm.

"He had symptoms of having taken an antidepressant. We've administered activated charcoal. Fortunately, your sitter noticed his breathing and heart rate and called right away."

"Antidepressants? Michelle doesn't have antidepressants in her house. I don't either." There was no way for him to get any.

"The EMTs brought in what was left of a brownie he'd eaten just before collapsing. It contained more than enough antidepressant to kill him if he'd eaten all of it, and not received medical attention."

Kayli covered her mouth. "He almost died?"

The doctor touched her arm. "Far from it. He didn't eat much. The EMT said the sitter told him Michael had gotten distracted before eating all of it."

"So, he really is okay?" Her shoulders relaxed.

"Yes. We're giving him fluids to keep him hydrated and monitoring his heart, which has been normal for the last twenty minutes."

"Can I see him?" She needed more than words to reassure her.

"Of course. Follow me."

He left Kayli at Michael's door. She stared into the room for a few seconds. Her little boy had just turned four and thought he was almost a man, but now he looked so small in the bed. If not for the tube coming from his hand, and extra pale skin, she'd think he was sleeping.

She crept to the bed and ran her fingers through his soft,

blond hair. He looked so much like his father, with a slight dip in his chin and the dimples when he smiled. He had her brown eyes, but they were wider, like his father's.

She took his little hand in her fingers, hands that rarely were idle. It was cooler than usual, so she tucked it under the blanket.

"Michael, Mommy's here. You're going to be fine." Her fingers brushed through his hair again. She loved doing it, but he didn't put up with it often anymore.

"I came so close to losing you, too. Who did this?" Now that Kayli had seen for herself that Michael wasn't in distress, she marched to the nurse's station. "Can you call the police for me? I think someone tried to kill my son."

The nurse's mouth dropped open before she quickly recovered. "Actually, they've already been called. We have to in cases like this. Why don't you go back to your son's room and I'll send them in when they get here?"

"Thank you." Kayli went back to Michael's room and paced. It was the first she'd noticed the large decals on the walls of puppies, kittens and bunnies. Not such a sterile room, but it still wasn't home. She was too wired to sit, but each turn brought her back to Michael to touch his arm, his hand, his face.

After twenty minutes, a dark skinned man in a neat, black suit knocked on the partially closed door, and walked into the room. "Mrs. McAllister?"

Kayli gripped the rail on the bed with both hands. "That's me. Are you with the police?"

"I'm Detective Barnes." He showed her his badge. "Why don't we go down to the waiting room so we don't disturb your son, and you can tell me why someone would try to kill him."

She stared down at Michael and bit her lip. She didn't feel safe leaving him. "Can we talk just outside the door? I

5

don't want to be far from him."

"Of course." The detective pulled the door mostly closed behind them.

She didn't know if he'd believe her. She clenched her hands at her sides. "The doctor told me that Michael had ingested antidepressant in a brownie."

"I saw that in his chart. Do you know who would do that?"

"No, but I found this on my car windshield this morning." Kayli reached into her purse and pulled out an envelope.

Detective Barnes pulled on disposable gloves and took the envelope by its edges. *Kayli* was laser-printed across the front in a large scrolled font. He pulled a page from it, and touching only corners, opened it and scanned the text.

I hope your birthday is as good as the one you had three years ago!

Your love belongs to me.

It was not signed.

"And how does this tell you that someone wanted to harm your son, Mrs. McAllister? It sounds innocuous." He carefully refolded the paper and returned it to the envelope, then slipped it into a plastic bag from his pocket.

"Today is my birthday. Three years ago on my birthday, my husband died."

Barnes frowned. "I'm sorry to hear that. He was poisoned also?"

"No. A speeding car veered off the street. I screamed for Max to move, but he didn't have time. It sped up just before it hit him." The scene played in her head like so many nightmares.

She closed her eyes and took a deep breath. She'd cried enough already. Strength was needed for Michael. Another deep breath. The tears prickled her eyes, and she reached into her pocket for a tissue and wiped them away. She tipped her head back, blinking at the ceiling. She'd had lots of experience keeping the tears under control.

She leveled her eyes on the detective. "The car didn't stop. The police found it eight blocks away, abandoned. The police told me it had been stolen, and assumed it was a teenager joyriding in a fancy sports car, who then panicked. They never believed me that it was intentional. I don't think they tried hard enough to find the killer."

"This note certainly sounds like the writer knew what happened on that other birthday, and it's suspicious that your son almost died today, too." He gave her his card. "I need to get contact information from you and for your sitter, and I'll have this note checked for fingerprints and trace evidence." He tucked the plastic enclosed envelope into his pocket. "We'll have to get a copy of your prints to rule yours out. Do you have any idea why someone is targeting your loved ones?"

"No." She bit her lip. "Up until today, I thought Max was a random, convenient target. I didn't realize that *he* was the target."

"I'm sorry nobody solved your husband's case. In light of this new evidence, I'll reopen it."

"Thank you." Maybe now, the murderer would be found.

Detective Barnes left and Kayli hurried to her son's side. When the killer found he wasn't successful, would he try again?

Chapter 2

Kayli woke and stretched the kinks out of her upper back. She opened her eyes and froze, for a second forgetting where she was. Her eyes darted around the room, taking in the animals on the wall and the hospital bed. The nightmare was real. She pushed down the footrest of the recliner and hurried to her son.

His color was back to normal and he looked as he always did when she checked on him before he woke. She touched his soft cheek. His eyes fluttered open. "Mommy." His eyes darted to the side and widened. She didn't want him to be frightened because he wasn't in his own bed.

Kayli leaned down and kissed his forehead. "Hi, honey. How do you feel?"

"My tummy hurts a little bit."

"Do you know what happened?" a stern voice said from the doorway.

Kayli gasped and straightened up.

"I'll take it from here, Mrs. McAllister." For such a large man, he was silent on his feet.

"Detective—I'm sorry. I've forgotten your name."

"Barnes."

"Detective Barnes, can't you wait until he's better to question him?"

"No. We need to do this while it's still fresh in his mind. Don't worry. I have three young children myself. I'll be gentle."

She stayed at Michael's side, with the man on the other.

She remained a lioness protecting her cub.

Detective Barnes pulled a chair up close to the bed on the opposite side from Kayli. It put him on eye level with Michael.

Kayli took her son's hand. "Michael, this is Detective Barnes. He's a policeman. He has some questions for you about yesterday. Can you talk to him?"

Michael nodded solemnly and turned to the detective.

"Hi, Michael. You can call me Al. Is it okay if I ask you some questions?" His voice had quieted. Michael nodded.

"How old are you?"

Michael held up four fingers. "I'm four." He looked over at Kayli. "Mommy, Michy made you a really pretty cake. I got to put chocolate chips on the top. And we have presents for you." He occasionally still used his nickname for Michelle from when he couldn't pronounce the letter l.

Kayli squeezed Michael's hand. "That sounds wonderful. We'll have to have cake after your tummy is better."

"Michael," Al said, "I hear you had a brownie yesterday. Can you tell me where you got it?"

"From Mommy."

Kayli gasped. "Honey, I didn't give you a brownie for your snack yesterday." The detective sent her a frown.

Michael turned to her. "Mommy, the man said you forgot to give it to me."

Tears sprang to Kayli's eyes as she looked at the detective. She blinked them away.

"Michael," Al said. When the boy turned back to him, he continued. "Where were you when the man gave you the brownie?"

"On the playground."

"Which playground?"

"At preschool." He pushed himself to a sitting position.

9

Al jotted in his notebook. "What did you do with the brownie?"

"I put it in my pocket. I already had my other snack."

"When did you eat the brownie?"

"At Michelle's."

"Did you know the man? Had you seen him before?" Michael shook his head. "Can you tell me what he looked like?"

"He had on a baseball hat."

"What color was it?"

"Black."

"Did you see his eyes?"

Michael nodded.

"What color were they?"

His eyes darted to Kayli. "Brown, like Mommy's."

"Did he wear glasses?"

The boy shook his head.

"Did he have a beard or mustache?"

Again the boy shook his head.

"Was his skin light like your mom's or dark like mine, or in between?"

His eyes bounced from the detective to his mother and back. "In between." Al wrote in his book.

"Did he have curly or straight hair?"

Michael shook his head and shrugged.

"Was the man wearing a coat?" At Michael's nod, he asked, "A long coat or short?"

Michael ran a hand across just below his hips.

"What color was the coat?"

"Black."

"Is there anything else you can think of about the man?"

The boy shrugged.

"Thank you, Michael. You did a good job." He looked up at Kayli. "Mrs. McAllister, could I see you in the hall?"

"Sure, Detective." Kayli stood and leaned over Michael. "I'll be right back." When she stepped outside the room, Barnes closed the door.

"What preschool does Michael go to?" She told him the name and address. "Does it have video surveillance of the playground?"

"I don't know. I've never noticed."

"I'll check it out. It's fortunate Michelle acted so quickly. I'd like to talk to her in case she can tell us more about this brownie. She's your sitter?"

"She's also my best friend." A friend who would get a present for saving Michael's life.

"Could I get her full name and number?" Kayli gave them to him and he thanked her. "I'd recommend that you have Michael stay with someone out of town until we find this guy. We don't know if he'll make another attempt."

She clutched her hand at her throat. She hadn't thought about hiding Michael. "He could stay with my mother."

"It might be better if it was your husband's relative. Since you're the ultimate target, he may already know where your mother lives."

She didn't want her mother to become a target. This man might try to take away another person she loved.

Max's brothers lived in town, so would be too close. Maybe Michelle's sister would take him. They'd gotten on well when she and her son had stayed with Michelle last year.

"Call me if Michael remembers anything else." Then he left.

Kayli checked the time as she walked back into Michael's room. Any other day, she'd already be at the office.

Kayli grabbed her purse from beside the recliner. "Michael, I'm going to go freshen up." She pointed to the bathroom. She needed to make a couple calls that she didn't want her son to hear. She pulled out her phone and dialed her secretary at the office. The call was picked up after two rings. "Higgins and Harper. Kayli—"

"Monica, it's Kayli."

"Kayli, is everything all right?"

Kayli ran her hand through her hair and was stopped by a tangle, which reminded her that she hadn't looked in a mirror that day. "Michael's in the hospital. Someone poisoned him." The words choked her. She could so easily have lost him.

"Oh, my God, Kayli. Is he okay?" Kayli brought Michael in every once in a while and Monica enjoyed his visits.

"Fortunately, Michelle knew right away it was serious. He's going to be fine."

"Thank God. I can't believe it. Who would do that to sweet little Michael?"

"I wish I knew. Anyway, I called to let you know that I won't be in today and to have you reschedule my appointments to the day after tomorrow or later."

"Of course, No problem."

Kayli ended the call and dialed again.

"Kayli, how's Michael?" Her friend's voice was a balm to her jumpy nerves.

"Thanks to your quick action, he's fine." She should have called her friend last night, but it had been too overwhelming.

"Good. When is he coming home?"

"That's the thing. I can't bring him home. Someone tried to kill him and I don't know if he'll try again."

"Oh, Kayli. Do you want him to stay here?" Always willing to help.

"No. This guy knows too much. He'd probably check your house. I was hoping you could convince Jackie to take him for a bit. They got on well when she visited."

"I'm sure she'd love it. Dom's been asking her to bring him back. I'm sure half that is so he can see Michael again."

"Thanks. I thought we could meet at the mall, and I can hand him over to you. You can park in the back. That way, if I'm followed, he'll see me leave in front. I'm just not sure if we should go home to pack a bag for him."

"No. Don't. Dom's clothes should fit well enough. And I won't go home until I've met up with Jackie."

Kayli let out an audible breath. "Thank you. You're the best friend ever."

"Of course. Food court at noon?"

"Perfect." Kayli dropped her phone into her purse with a lighter heart. It would be hard to have Michael away for an indeterminate length of time, but he'd be safe.

She scrounged in her purse for her brush, and found a business card, with no clue how it had gotten there. *Shawn Gordon, Private Investigations and Security.* She hadn't picked up a PI's card. Then it dawned on her that the man on the bike she had collided with had given her his card. She stuffed it back in her purse and reached deeper to pull out her brush. Once she was presentable, she opened the door.

"Mommy?"

Kayli walked over to the bed and laid her hand on his arm. "Yes, honey?"

"Are we going to go home soon? I don't like it here."

She plastered an excited smile on her face. "Michelle just told me that Dom has been asking about you and his mom invited you to stay with them for a few days. What do you think?"

"Yes! Dom is fun. His house will have more boy toys than Kim's house."

She chuckled. "You're probably right."

His mind had been taken off the detective and his recent experiences. She didn't want to explain that someone had

13

tried to hurt him.

Chapter 3

Kayli worried that the man who gave the brownie to Michael would show up at the hospital. She had wanted to leave as soon as Detective Barnes finished talking to Michael, but they were on hospital time. Another two hours passed before the doctor came in and checked Michael out. "Hey, champ. You're doing great. You ready to go home?"

"I'm not going home. I'm—"

Kayli put her hand over Michael's mouth and leaned close to him. "It's a surprise." He nodded and she removed her hand. She couldn't take a chance that the wrong person would hear.

The doctor raised his brows. "I'll have the nurse bring the discharge papers." He left.

Kayli helped Michael get dressed, and by the time they were finished, the nurse came in with a handful of papers and a wheelchair.

"I can see someone's anxious to leave."

Michael beamed. "Yes. I—" He sucked in his lips at Kayli's wide eyes.

The nurse chuckled and placed the papers on the lap tray. "I need you to read these and sign the bottom." She placed a pen beside the papers.

Kayli scanned and signed the papers. She was as anxious as Michael to leave.

The nurse picked up the papers. "All right, little man. Hop into your ride."

Michael eyed the wheelchair. "That's for babies."

The nurse laughed. "Nope. Everybody leaves this way. Even your mom did when you were born."

He stared wide eyed at Kayli.

"That's right. I sat in a wheelchair with you in my arms and your dad pushed us out to the car." She would not tear up.

The nurse must have noticed her reaction. "Hop up, little man."

He climbed into the chair and placed his arms on the armrests, which were much too high, then he moved them to his lap. The nurse pushed the chair into the hallway and Kayli followed behind. In the elevator, Kayli scooted close to the nurse. "When we get to the door, can you stay inside with Michael until I bring the car up?"

The woman's brow wrinkled and then her eyes widened. She must have remembered that Kayli had asked her to call the police. "Yes, of course."

Outside, Kayli hurried to her car and brought it around to the door. Were they being watched? Not likely, but knowing there were other times they'd been observed sent shivers up her spine.

The wheelchair came out. Kayli jumped from the car and opened the back door, shielding Michael as she helped him into his seat and buckled him in. She closed the door and thanked the nurse.

At the mall, Kayli insisted on carrying Michael, so they could get inside more quickly. They entered through a store, and once they reached the hall outside it, Kayli lowered her son to the floor. "Okay, let's go to the food court."

He grabbed her hand and pulled. "Yay. I want a hamburger and French fries."

His little stomach must have recovered. "I don't think you should have fries today."

At the entrance to the food court, his head swiveled from

one end to the other. He pointed at a sub shop. "Can I have meatballs?"

It was his second favorite food at the mall. "All right."

With the food purchased, she chose a seat where she could watch both entrances. She didn't know who she was watching for besides Michelle. It was nearly noon, so it wouldn't be long.

She cut the meatballs into bite size pieces and Michael began eating. Between bites, he talked about all the things he wanted to do with Dom.

They had nearly finished their meal when Kayli spotted Michelle as she paused at the edge of the food court. Kayli waved and Michelle started towards them.

Kayli hugged her friend, not letting go for way too long. "You saved him. I can't even think about what would have happened. Forever, thank you." She gave an extra squeeze before releasing her.

"I'm just glad it wasn't as bad as it looked." She pointed to a hamburger stand. "I'll grab some food and eat on the road."

"I thought you would have picked up Kim on your way."

Michelle shook her head. "I'd hoped that Jackie could meet me halfway, but she had an appointment. I'm driving all the way and staying overnight. Donny will leave work early to pick up Kim from school and get her there in the morning."

Kayli gripped her friend's hand. "I didn't mean to cause all this trouble."

"Hey. What are best friends for? You'd do the same for me."

"I would, but I've been doing most of the taking over the last few years."

"Uh-uh. Look how many date nights you've let us have. Kim thinks we plan these overnights for her. Little does she know that Mommy and Daddy get to play, too."

They'd had lots of double dates from high school on, but the year Michael and Kim were born, they hadn't wanted to leave them with anyone else. They'd taken turns watching each others baby so the other couple could go out. Of course, they'd still gotten together at both their houses. It wasn't the same anymore since they were no longer two couples.

"All right. Let me go grab a meal and we can get out of here."

She hurried to a burger stand.

Michael pushed his empty bowl away. "What games do Michy and Donny play?"

"Games?" She thought he'd been people watching and not paying attention to their conversation. "Oh. You know the top shelf in the toy closet? That has games for adults to play."

Just then, Michelle returned. "I'm ready." She held out her hand to Michael. "Big guy, are you ready to go see Dom?"

He jumped out of his seat and took her hand, then pulled it away. "Bye, Mommy." He wrapped his arms as far as he could around her middle.

She lifted him into her lap and hugged him. She hoped it wouldn't be too long before she had him back home. "I love you."

"I love you, too." He patted her cheek and kissed it. Then he jumped off her lap and took Michelle's hand.

She stayed in her seat. After a few steps, Michael turned and waved. She forced a smile and waved back. They disappeared around the turn before she had the strength to leave.

She'd known Jackie nearly as long as Michelle, but it was still hard letting him go. He'd be safer away from her. She couldn't help thinking that, even without killing Michael, this man had succeeded in taking her son from her.

Chapter 4

Already the house felt empty and too quiet. Nothing like when Michael spent the night with Kim. She prowled around and found the stuffed dinosaur, Ralph, on the couch in the living room. She hugged it and remembered his excitement when he found it in the science museum store six months ago. His teddy bear had been relegated to the toy chest ever since.

She wished she'd been able to get Ralph and clothes for Michael. Beside her son's bed, Kayli dropped down with the dinosaur tucked into her neck, not having the strength to hold back the tears. When Max died, the only thing that kept her going was Michael. And to keep Michael safe, she had to move forward, do what needed to be done. Deep breaths helped calm her. She wiped her cheeks, then carefully tucked Ralph under the blankets, like she would have with Michael.

Kayli paced through the first floor rooms. Everywhere there were signs of her son. It would be hard to live with him away for who knew how long. He was the only reason she had been able to go on when Max was killed. For a short time after his death, she'd become obsessed with Michael's safety. It turned out there was reason for that feeling.

Kayli was so relieved that Michelle had realized the seriousness of Michael's sudden pain. She wouldn't have been able to go on living if he'd died, which is what made it marginally easier to live with the separation. He was safe, but it was hard to not hear his little voice and have him wrap his arms around her. That little smile, so much like his father's, tugged at her heart every time.

A thought struck her and she stopped pacing. Maybe that private investigator could help out. He might be able to assist Al Barnes in finding this killer so she could have Michael home sooner. She pulled the card from her purse and called the number.

A woman answered. "Gordon Private Investigations. How may I help you?"

"Hi, I'd like to speak with Shawn Gordon. I'm Kayli McAllister, but he'll remember me as the woman who collided with him yesterday." She'd barely looked at him. Couldn't pick him out of a lineup. Maybe he hadn't told his assistant about their collision.

"Just a moment." The line went silent.

A vaguely familiar deep voice filled the void. "Kayli McAllister. There's a name to go with the face. Are you more injured than you thought?" His voice was gentle. He'd probably nurtured it to calm stressed clients. It was already helping her collect her thoughts.

"Ah, oh, no. I'm fine. I need to talk to a private investigator, and I just found your card. My son was nearly killed and I had to send him away to keep him safe. I hope you can help me find who did this so I can bring him home. Do you have any time to squeeze me in?"

"Let me check with my secretary. Hold on." Music played for a minute, and Shawn came back on. "Can you make four o'clock?"

It wouldn't be a long wait. "Thank you. I'll see you then."

~~~

"Have a seat, Ms. McAllister." Shawn pointed to the chair in front of his desk. The late afternoon sunlight turned her wavy hair a golden brown. It cascaded just past her shoulders. He didn't think he'd ever see the beautiful woman again. The panic was gone, but the deep brown eyes now held so much sadness.

Her eyes went to his empty gun holster and widened a little. He kept his gun in his desk while in the office, but wanted to assure clients that he would be armed.

"Thank you. Please call me Kayli." She perched on the chair. "Cost isn't an issue. The most important thing is my son's safety."

"We can discuss a retainer later. So, why do you need a PI?"

She pulled in a deep breath. "Yesterday morning when my son and I were leaving home, there was an envelope on my windshield. It said, *I hope your birthday is as good as the one you had three years ago. Your love belongs to me.*"

"I take it that wasn't a good birthday for you?" Shawn asked.

"No." He didn't think it was possible, but her eyes grew bleaker. "My husband died."

"I'm sorry. It must have been especially hard on your birthday. Can you tell me how it happened?" He kept his voice gentle, not wanting to sound like an interrogator. He jotted notes as she answered.

"It was a hit and run. We were having lunch at a street cafe." She described what happened. "He died in my arms."

A box of tissue sat on the corner of his desk and she snatched one. He waited, giving her time to recover. To lose a husband she loved deeply was traumatic, but to see him murdered in front of her had to have taken a huge toll. He admired her courage to pick up the pieces and reassemble her life.

"And they didn't find who did it?" She would have given a name, if she'd known, but he needed to make sure.

"No. They thought it was a joyriding teenager who panicked. I don't think they tried very hard. But I know that car sped up as it got closer. My husband was murdered." Her words started softly, but increased in intensity, until she finished with anger. She'd need that anger to help her son.

Shawn leaned forward, his hands on the desk. "So, what happened yesterday?"

"My four year old son was poisoned." Tears shimmered in Kayli's eyes.

"Is he all right?" With all he'd seen, it was still hard to accept that there were people who would kill children.

"Yes, thank God. My sitter acted quickly."

Shawn remembered Kayli telling someone to call for an ambulance "Your son was with the sitter. What's her name and number?"

"Michelle Meade." She gave the number.

"What did she tell you?"

"Michelle said that within minutes of having his snack, Michael was writhing on the floor in pain. Thank God he didn't finishing that brownie. Michelle called me right away. Remembering the note from that morning, I knew that it was serious and had her call for an ambulance."

"Where is Michael now?"

Kayli's bit her lip. "Um."

"It's okay. Even if I don't take your case, what you tell me is confidential."

"My sitter is my best friend. We've known each other since grade school. He's with her sister, Jackie. She lives a few hours away."

"That sounds perfect."

Her eyes glistened and she blinked several times. Of course, it wasn't perfect for her. First her son almost died, and then she had to send him away.

"I'm sorry he's had to go through this. Both of you."

23

"I need you to find this man so I can safely bring my son back home." She dabbed her eyes. "I wish I would have thought of a private investigator after my husband died."

"You do realize that this man is doing this to get to you somehow."

"What do you mean?"

"Maybe he's taking away those you love to cause you emotional pain. Maybe he thinks you'll turn to him for comfort."

"All along, I thought Max was a random easy target, like for a gang's initiation. Now with this note, I realize that someone wanted to kill *him*." Her hands trembled, and she wrapped them around the arms of the chair. It didn't help. "But, why wait three years?"

"He may have thought he'd have a chance with you with your husband gone and was giving you time to fall for him. Or maybe he's been away until recently. Is there anyone who's shown romantic interest in you lately?"

She shrugged. "I don't think so. If the conversation starts to get too personal, I cut it off."

"Why don't you think about it a bit more and let me know."

"I'm more scared now than when I came here. I didn't think about why this happened."

"I don't mean to frighten you, but you do have to be careful. You're a target. For whatever reason, he's proven he'll do anything to get near you."

"I know you're right, but what do I do?"

"Exactly what you're doing. You came to exactly the right place. I'm good at my job. I'll make sure nothing more happens to you." He pulled out a notepad and pen. "Now, tell me how Michael got the poison."

Kayli described the conversation with Detective Barnes while Shawn took notes.

"I worked with Al for a short time. I'll give him a call and see if you can view the surveillance footage from the school. You may recognize the guy."

She nodded.

"I'd like to talk to Michelle, also."

"I just thought of something. Michelle's daughter goes to the same preschool. She picks both kids up and takes them back to her house. I wonder if Kim saw the man, too."

"Good point. I'll ask when I talk to her. Now let's go back to your husband's murder. If he was the target, how did this guy find him?"

"Once a week we met for lunch, and if the weather was nice, it was at our favorite cafe with outdoor seating. We always met on Wednesdays, but that week, we actually delayed it a day so we'd lunch together on my birthday."

"Hmmm. I wonder if he drove by on Wednesday," Shawn speculated. "He didn't find the two of you, so tried again the next day. That would mean that he stole a car each day or he kept a stolen car overnight. Or maybe he somehow knew you changed the day. Did you tell anyone about the different day?"

Kayli wrinkled her brow. "I don't think so," she said slowly. "Oh, wait. I had lunch with my secretary on Wednesday instead, so she knew. And we stopped to talk to a few people on our way out."

"And their names?" He poised his pen above the paper.

"I really don't remember."

"Maybe your secretary remembers who you talked to, or if she told anyone."

"Ok. I'll ask. Anything else?"

"What about social media? Are you on any of those sites?"

"I post pictures of Michael and what he's doing on Facebook. But it's set to show to only family and close friends." She bit her lip. Now, she felt guilty about posting to Facebook.

"It's probably fine, but don't post anything more until this is resolved."

"It's not like I have anything I want to post, anyway."

"That should do it for now. You'll talk to your secretary. I'll talk to Michelle and Detective Barnes, and I'll call you tomorrow afternoon. Hopefully, I'll have more information and an appointment for you to look at the video."

Kayli stood. "Thank you. I wish this guy would disappear again, but I have a feeling he's not done with me yet."

Chapter 5

Her first day back to work after Michael's poisoning, Kayli wasn't sure if she'd be able to concentrate. She walked through the main office area and Dave Peters stopped her.

"Hey, Kayli. I heard at the monthly meeting that your son was in the hospital. How's he doing?"

Kayli wished she'd thought to tell Monica not to mention it. Dave was the last person she wanted to talk with. "Hi, Dave. He was in overnight, but he's fine now." Kayli tried to ignore the way Dave's gaze always strayed to her breasts. It was more disconcerting than usual with the serious subject. When his gaze reached her face, there was no concern for her son.

Could this man be responsible for hurting her Michael and killing Max? He was a creep, but she couldn't picture him as a killer.

"I can give you the rundown on the meeting," he said.

"That's all right. I'll read through the minutes that Janice sends out."

Nancy, a woman she chatted with occasionally, came up and put an arm around Kayli. "I'm so sorry to hear about Michael. How is he?" At least she sounded sincere.

"He's out of the hospital and he's fine now."

"What happened?" Nancy liked to tell everybody about her kids, from colds to home runs. No surprise that she was curious about Michael.

"I really don't want to talk about it."

The woman stiffened and dropped her arm. "Well I'm

glad he's doing better. Let me know if I can do anything."

"Thanks, Nancy."

The woman returned to her desk and Kayli was alone again with Dave. "Well, I've got work to catch up on, so I'll see you later." Kayli hurried to the elevator and hoped the doors would open soon. She could feel Dave staring at her and suppressed a shiver.

Since her client visits had been postponed, she had plenty of time to catch up. Kayli worked on a presentation for a new client. The basics of how an ad agency could help them just needed some tweaking for their specific needs. She would have to learn more about their market before she could complete it. A job for Monica.

Shawn called mid afternoon. "Can you meet with Al Barnes at the police station at 4:00?"

"Yes, I can do that. Are you going to be there?"

"Yes. I have some things to discuss with you afterward."

~~~

Kayli walked into the police station just before four o'clock and spotted a grim looking Shawn talking to a uniformed officer. He introduced her to his brother, Kyle. She was surprised they were related since they looked nothing alike. Kyle's hair was dark, almost black. His eyes were the deepest brown. Kayli looked from one to the other.

Shawn noticed and chuckled. "Kyle looks like our mother and I take after our father." Shawn told Kyle he'd see him later and led Kayli to Al's cubicle.

Al, hunched over his desk, typing with two fingers. Two stacks of papers were to his left, and a picture on his right, with the back facing her. Wife or children? He glanced up, and rolled his chair back, stood and shook Shawn's hand. "I was surprised when I got your call, Shawn." His eyes cut to

Kayli. "Nice to see you, Mrs. McAllister."

She hoped he didn't think she hired Shawn because she thought he couldn't solve the case. "Call me Kayli."

"Thanks for seeing us," Shawn said.

"Shawn, pull a couple of chairs around to this side of my desk. I've got the surveillance on my computer."

Then Shawn, Al, and Kayli faced the monitor, where two, slightly overlapping, views of the playground were frozen. The video started just before the image of a man walk up to the fence at the preschool. He pulled something from his left coat pocket.

"I've zoomed in on that, but I can't make out what it is," Al said.

On the other half of the screen, a boy pushed another boy to the ground. Tears streaked the fallen boy's face, but he appeared to be yelling at the boy standing over him. A teacher rushed to the boys and squatted beside the one on the ground. The other teacher took the other boy aside and leaned down, talking to him. Most of the children gathered around one or the other of the teachers.

Al pointed to the man. "Whatever he held, he stuffed it back in his pocket. I bet he was going to use it for a distraction, but he didn't need it. Now, he's speaking. Probably calling out to Michael. Notice how both teachers have their backs to the guy.

"I can't see his face," Kayli said.

"He knows the cameras are there," Al said.

He must have planned ahead of time where he could stand and how to face.

The man wore a black, leather coat with the collar turned up. A baseball cap, with the brim pulled low, sat on his head.

They watched as Michael turned toward the guy. Then the boy took a few steps toward him and stopped. The man talked more and held out his hand with something in it.

Michael stepped closer and nodded, then took a plastic bag from the man and shoved it into his pocket. He looked at the man for a couple of seconds, then ran back to join the group of children around the fallen boy. The man turned and walked away.

"Kayli, do you recognize him?" Al asked.

She shook her head. "I don't know who he is. With the coat to hide his body and the hat low over his face, there isn't much to identify."

"Does he seem at all familiar? The way he stands or walks? Anything?"

"No. I wish he did. Can you replay just that camera view?" Now that she knew she wouldn't see his face, maybe something else would catch her eye. She leaned forward and clenched her hands. There had to be something.

It played through again and she watched every move the man made. As he approached the fence, and pulled the mysterious item from his pocket. As he returned it, which she'd missed last time, and as he squatted down to Michael's level, and then as he walked out of the shot. Nothing. She shook her head. "No. I still don't recognize him."

"Don't worry about it," the detective said. "It was a long shot. We're still coming up to speed on this." He stood and the others followed. "I'll let you know if I get any more information or have more questions."

"Al, I took your advice and sent Michael away."

"I know this is hard on you, but it's best for Michael."

"Knowing that was the only reason I could do it."

~~~

Shawn took Kayli to a nearby restaurant and sat across from her. They ordered coffee and spinach artichoke dip with chips. After the server brought their coffee, Shawn picked up his cup and set it down without drinking.

"Kayli, I think we need to create a show." He'd gone over all the information she'd given him and talked to Al. No one stood out as a suspect.

Her eyebrows dropped. "What do you mean?"

"I'd like to leak out that your son got taken away because you're a suspect in his poisoning."

"But that's not true!"

"No, but I'm hoping the stalker will think this makes you more vulnerable, and he'll make a mistake."

Kayli gasped.

Shawn touched her hand. "Anybody who knows you will know that you didn't do it. Even the stalker knows you didn't do it."

She sighed. "I don't know how that's going to help, but if this can get Michael home sooner, then I'll go along with it."

"Okay. We'll wait about three days, and make it look like we're dating." Shawn watched Kayli carefully. This would be the more difficult task to get her to agree to. Michelle had told him that Kayli hadn't dated since her husband's death. He'd asked in case a man in her life might be responsible. Which was true, but he'd wanted to the answer for himself, too.

She withdrew her hand from his. Sadness was back in her eyes, this time from the loss of her husband.

"I don't know if I can do that." Her gaze remained riveted her hand, so near his.

"It's all make-believe, Kayli."

"I know, but...but..." Suddenly her voice grew stronger. "What about you? He'll know it's a setup because you're a PI."

"That's the easy part. I have another identity set up where I work at my oldest brother's business, *Suncrest Realty*

31

Company. I occasionally do work on his computers under that other name. So I've got good enough credentials and business cards. I can actually go to 'the office'. Even the admin thinks I work there."

"That's convenient. What's your other name?"

"Shawn Williams. It's up to you. Are you willing to try this?"

"How will that help?"

"It may draw him out to try to eliminate me."

"No!" She looked around as heads turned toward her. Then she whispered, "You can't do that. I don't want someone else to die because of me."

"You're not the cause, and it's not as dangerous as it seems. I have the advantage of knowing I may be a target, and I'm trained to take care of myself."

Kayli studied him, then sighed. "All right. It's probably the fastest way to finish this."

Shawn smiled. "Now, tomorrow, I want you to reveal to your secretary that your son was taken from you. Don't tell her to not tell anyone. We want it to get around. Is there anyone else you could tell who might spread it faster?"

Kayli frowned. "I should tell my boss. It's something I would tell him if it was true. He shouldn't hear it through the grapevine. But I don't think that's going to help our cause. I'll have to tell Michelle what we're doing."

"Do you think that's wise?"

"She's been my best friend since middle school. Her husband, Donny was my husband, Max's, best friend. We double dated through high school and college. We even had a double wedding. She can be trusted to keep my secrets."

Shawn raised his hands as if to hold her off. "Okay, okay. Why don't you tell her to let it slip about you being a suspect to a neighbor or other friends?"

"She wouldn't normally do that, but I'll see what she

says. Oh, there's Nancy at work. She always knows everything about everybody. I'm sure if I let it slip to her, it won't take long for everybody to know."

"I'll call Al to let him know what we're doing. He's going to blow his stack and tell me I'm putting you in danger, but he doesn't anything to go on yet. If this works, he'll appreciate it." Shawn would do his best to make sure that any danger was on his shoulders and didn't touch Kayli.

Chapter 6

Mid morning, Kayli stood up from her desk. It was time to put her acting skills to work. This was for Michael. It had to work. She picked up papers for Monica and took a cleansing breath. "Here goes," she whispered.

She walked toward her secretary's desk. "Monica, here's the report for Jason. Can you look it over—" It slipped out of her fingers just before Monica could take hold of it. The sheets hit the edge of the desk and scattered over the floor. "Darn! Another thing goes wrong." She ran her fingers through her hair.

Monica jumped up from her chair and rushed to retrieve the sheets. She frowned. "Kayli, is everything all right?"

"Yes. No." She ran her fingers through her hair again. "That police detective is considering me as a suspect in Michael's poisoning. He had social services take Michael to protect him. From me."

"What! No way. Anyone who knows you knows how much you love that little boy." Monica straightened the papers and set them on her desk. She laid her hand on Kayli's arm. "They should be able to figure out soon enough that you didn't do it. If it will help, I'll talk to the detective."

Kayli massaged her temples. "Thanks for your support. It helps. I had to tell Bill this morning. That was no picnic. It would have looked really bad if the boss learned about it from someone else."

"That sucks. Was he okay with it?"

"Yeah. He was as shocked as you. I miss Michael

already, but then I remember that someone tried to kill him and I'm glad he's hidden away." She looked at Monica with tears shimmering in her eyes and blinked a few times to try to clear them. It was easy to play the part when the pain was real.

"Maybe you should go home," Monica suggested.

"I can't. If I'm home all alone, it would be worse. Besides, I've got another presentation to work up by the end of the day. It will be a much needed distraction."

"My brother is joining me for lunch today. Why don't you come along?" Kayli saw the concern in Monica's eyes.

"No, but thanks. I wouldn't be good company. I brought a lunch, so I'll work through. Have fun and take extra time if you need it."

"Thanks. I've only seen John once since he got back two weeks ago."

"Oh, where's he been?"

"His company sent him to Los Angeles for about a year to straighten out production there. He only came back at Christmas time."

"Enjoy your lunch and don't worry about me." Kayli went back into her office. Monica had seemed convinced. Of course, half of what she said was the truth and all the emotional parts were true, so she really hadn't done a lot of acting.

She hoped Michael would have a good time with Dom and not get too homesick.

Concentrating on finding new clients to call helped push thoughts of Michael away, mostly. She added ten more to the list to make twenty. She copied half to another document and printed it out. Monica knew what information needed to be pulled together. She gave it one last look as she brought it to the other room. "Monica?"

She glanced up. A man sat on the edge of Monica's desk,

wearing jeans and a dark purple pullover—Monica's brother. They shared pale blue-gray eyes, hers with more lashes. His hair was shorter than she remembered, as if to rid it of the curls that softened his features.

"Oh." It was ten minutes before noon. "I hadn't realized it was so late."

He stood. "I don't know if you remember me—"

"Of course, John." Kayli held out her hand in greeting. He took it in both of his and she thought he would lift it to his lips and kiss it, but released her after a couple of seconds. He'd gone to lunch with Monica on a regular basis, and often stopped into office pick her up. "Monica told me you've just returned from the west coast."

"Yeah. I'm glad to be back home. It was nice that my company provided a furnished apartment, but it's good to be in my own place again. And around normal people. There are a lot of crazy people out there."

"Well, you two have a nice lunch and don't worry about the time." She turned to Monica. "When you get back, I have some research for you." She laid the list on Monica's desk.

"Why don't you join us?" John asked.

"No, not today. Maybe another time. It was nice seeing you, John." Kayli returned to her office. Could John be the one? He'd just returned from a year in California. One year, not three. Would she look at every man with suspicion now?

Chapter 7

Shawn took Kayli to one of his favorite restaurants for their first fake date. The atmosphere at *Mortimer Steakhouse* allowed for conversation, unlike the sports bars his brothers preferred. Kayli fidgeted as if she sat outside the principal's office at school, something in which he was familiar. He hadn't expected her to be so nervous. She scooted her chair closer to the table, touched her necklace, ran her hand over her hair, and adjusted the bracelet on her wrist. If he didn't know she was a widow, he'd think she'd never been out with a man before.

"This feels so weird," Kayli said, eying the other diners.

It couldn't be her appearance. Her jade green dress hugged her figure, and complimented the dark hair she'd swept up into soft curls. Maybe she felt someone watching. He'd requested a table next to the wall to have a good view of the room. He scanned, starting at the door, met a woman's eyes, and she looked away. Everyone else seemed focused on their companions, and there were no lone men. Her discomfort must have been focused on him.

He smiled at her. "Relax. We're just two people having dinner."

"I know, but the last man I shared dinner with was Max." She took a deep breath. "The last first date I had was in high school." She put her fingers over her mouth and blinked a few times. Her eyes dropped to the rings on her finger.

She'd married her high school sweetheart. No wonder she seemed so on edge. Besides her husband, she'd probably

37

not been alone with a man in ten years.

He gently covered her hand with his. It trembled slightly. "Consider us friends. You're having dinner with a friend. Now take a deep breath and open your menu." He withdrew his hand. Once she'd opened her menu, he smiled. "What kind of food do you like?"

"A nice tender steak. Maybe a filet mignon." Kayli raised nervous eyes to him.

"A woman after my own heart." Her smile faltered and he rushed to explain. "My favorite is usually steak, too."

Generally, he didn't drink on a job, but he wanted Kayli to relax, so he ordered a beer and encouraged her to order a drink also when they ordered their food. She ordered wine. He'd want to keep his wits so wouldn't drink it all.

Shawn talked about cases he'd worked on as a police detective. He kept it light and only told stories that had a funny angle. They were laughing over a case that involved boxes of stolen tennis balls when their food arrived.

"When we were at the police station yesterday," Kayli said, "you seemed to be on really good terms with Al Barnes. Did you used to work with him?"

"We were partners for about six months when I first made detective, while his partner convalesced from a bullet to the leg. Al and I became friends. We still meet for a beer once in a while."

"So, he's a good guy? He's going to help us find this man who hurt Michael?" Kayli caught her lip between her teeth.

"He's one of the best good guys. He'll do a thorough follow up on every lead he gets."

Kayli had stopped fidgeting. Hopefully, that meant she was more comfortable with him. He took a small sip of his beer and eyed her glass. Maybe the three-quarters of a glass of wine she'd finished had mellowed her.

"Tell me about Michael."

Her face lit up. "He's the sweetest boy. Rarely a temper tantrum. He's so independent."

"I bet he wants to do everything for himself."

She chuckled. "Oh, yes. A few days ago, I heard something fall in the bathroom. I went in and found toilet paper unrolled across the floor. Michael had tried to put on a fresh roll, but he couldn't compress the holder. It flew out of his hand and hit the wall. He was so upset that he couldn't do it." Her lips trembled. She must be remembering that she had to send her son away.

He had to distract her. "I was like that, too. I was probably a little older than Michael, when one day, I wanted something on a top shelf of my closet. I pulled one of my kid chairs into the closet, but it wasn't tall enough. Then I put a box on that, and I still couldn't reach. I added a couple of thick books from my dad's office, and climbed up. Stretching, I could just reach what I wanted, but something was on top of it. I tugged and a whole bunch of stuff fell. I was barely balanced as it was, so I tumbled down with everything landing on top of me. Mom rushed into my room. As soon as she made sure I wasn't hurt, I was grounded."

"But, it was an accident."

"Oh, I had multiple infractions. I definitely shouldn't have stacked all that stuff up. I took my dad's books. The toy I was after was taken away from me for a week and it had only been a couple of days."

Kayli covered her mouth and giggled. "Ah. Independent and a rule breaker."

He shrugged and grinned. "At least now, I'm more careful about what rules I break."

Her eyebrows rose. She wasn't a rule breaker.

The server placed apple pie alamode in front of them.

"We have to create our story," Shawn said.

"Story?"

"You can spread the word we're dating."

She nodded, but her fingers sought out her rings.

"Hey, I'm not a life sentence."

"Sorry. It's a big change for me." She folded her hands tightly together.

Shawn put his hand over her chilled ones. "You can do this." He'd never had to be so gentle with a client before. His job often required protecting his client, but he wanted to protect her from more than a killer.

She nodded and spread her hands flat on the table for a second before dropping them to her lap.

He cleared his throat. "First off, how about if we tell people we met at the food cart in front of your building? You can say we've been talking a couple times a week for several weeks, and I finally asked you out."

Kayli nodded. "That's plausible. Maybe we should meet at the cart occasionally to keep up the story."

Shawn smiled. He'd been about to make the suggestion. Now he wouldn't have to convince her.

"That's a good idea. How about day after tomorrow I'll meet you there? I'll buy you lunch, and we can eat on a bench in the park."

Kayli pressed her lips together. Surprising that now she seemed to regret her idea.

Shawn hurried on. "We have to be seen together to provoke a response. It's only a park. Not even a fake date."

Kayli nodded. "Okay. Friday at noon?"

"Perfect." Shawn paid the bill and led the way through the maze of tables.

She sighed behind him, and her hand slipped into his.

It startled him that she'd initiate a touch. He gave her hand a light squeeze, and raised his brows as he glanced over his shoulder. She had relaxed enough to play this game. He was beginning to wish it wasn't a game. He'd enjoyed their evening together.

"Gotta make it look real, right?" she asked and smiled.

He caught his breath. There was something different about that smile than when she laughed at dinner. He hoped he'd see it more. He turned back and continued out to the street. He hated having to release her hand when they got to his car.

There was little conversation on the way to her house. Maybe she'd had all she could take for one evening.

Shawn parked in the driveway beside Kayli's Camry, and walked her to her door. "Now we'll get close." He placed his hand on the side of her neck, his face inches from hers. "Anyone watching will think we've kissed. It *is* our first date, after all." His body urged him to press her back against the door, but he fought it. Her eyes closed, and he knew she'd accept his kiss, but he needed to keep this professional. It took a great deal of effort to move back from her.

She might have been a little dazed or maybe it was the wine.

He took a deep breath. Focus. "Those security signs do mean you really have an alarm system, don't they?"

"Yes, I do, and I always keep it on. Well, not the back door if Michael's running in and out." She bit her lip. She must be thinking that Michael won't be there to run in and out.

He touched her cheek. "Remember. We're doing this for Michael."

She nodded.

"Before I leave, I want to make sure you lock the door and set the alarm." She stepped inside, closed the door and both locks clicked. The alarm beeped as she entered her code.

"It's all set, Shawn. Thank you," she called through the door.

"Good night, Kayli." He scanned the street as he returned to his car. He drove passed two cars parked in front of neighboring houses. Unless someone had crouched down on his approach, the cars were unoccupied.

The evening might have been a wasted effort as far as getting the killer to notice him, but spending time with Kayli was no waste at all.

Chapter 8

Kayli breezed into her office with a smile on her face. She dropped a coffee pod into the machine and waited for it to brew. She could do this. She'd rehearsed all the way to work.

Monica gave her a puzzled look. "You're looking awfully chipper this morning."

"I had a date last night. It was the first since—" She closed her eyes for a second. "Anyway, I had a good time." Even with rehearsal, it was hard to talk about a date with someone that wasn't Max.

Monica smiled. "I'm glad for you. Do I know this guy?" She put her chin into her hand.

"I don't think so. His name is Shawn Williams. We've been running into each other at the food cart in front of the building. Tomorrow we're going to get food together at the cart and eat in the park." She frowned and said, "I hope it doesn't rain."

Monica chuckled. "I'm sure you'll work out something if it does. So, where did you go?"

"We went to *Mortimer's*. I'd forgotten how good their food is."

"I went there a couple weeks ago. Most boring date I ever had, but almost worth it for the food."

Kayli forced a smile. "Well, I wasn't bored. Shawn is nice. I'm sure he saw how nervous I was at first, and he sort of distracted me from it."

Monica squeezed her hand. "He *does* sound nice."

Kayli entered her office, set her coffee on her desk, then strode to the side of the room where Monica couldn't see her. She put her forehead against the books in the bookcase and closed her eyes. That had been so hard to do, to act excited about going out with someone who wasn't Max.

She *had* enjoyed herself, and at the same time, felt like she had betrayed Max. No matter how much she told herself it had been three years and he wouldn't want her to put the rest of her life on hold, she wasn't ready to let go. She stepped back and rubbed her temples. A deep breath settled her, and she sat at her desk to start her workday.

Her mind kept returning to the night before. After she'd gotten over the initial awkwardness, she enjoyed the evening with Shawn. She couldn't forget they were putting on a show because he frequently searched the room. But other than that, he was very attentive. He smiled a lot and somehow drew a few smiles from her.

She touched her fingers to her lips. He'd almost kissed her, and she'd wanted him to. Being so close to him brought back needs that she had long ago pushed out of her life.

~~~

The next day the sun shone brightly on Kayli's way to work. She hoped the planned lunch with Shawn would be wonderful. A pang of guilt reminded her how much she still loved Max, and that she shouldn't look forward to a pretend date. They weren't having a lunch date. They were trying to draw out a killer. This was almost a business transaction. She felt so confused. It had been better when she was numb.

No one stopped her on the way up to her office, and she'd gotten in ahead on Monica, for once.

She kept checking the clock, and no more than ten or fifteen minutes had past each time. That made for a long,

unproductive morning, but she couldn't be late meeting
Shawn. Her stomach tightened. Then an image of those blue
eyes smiling at her caused her clenched stomach to burst into
butterflies.

A flash caught her eye when she put her left hand on the
desk. Her wedding and engagement rings. She'd never felt
able to remove them. They were a loving reminder of the
man who'd given them to her. She spun them around.

Monica walked in with a folder and her eyes narrowed
on Kayli's hands. "Are you okay? You look a little green."

"Dating again is so hard. I feel guilty. Then I tell myself
I shouldn't." She held up her hand. "And what must Shawn
think of me still wearing my rings? But I'm not ready to take
them off yet." She dropped her forehead into her palm.

Monica set the folder down and pulled a chair to the side
of the desk. She touched Kayli's arm. "He knows you're a
widow?"

Kayli nodded.

"So he knows you're not cheating on a husband. He
probably suspects that you had a very good marriage and that
you're having a hard time letting go. Just do what feels right
for you, Kayli."

Kayli stared into Monica's eyes, seeing all the concern
and worry. She put her hand on Monica's. "Thank you."

"Now," Monica said in a brighter voice. "It's almost
noon. You should go powder your nose and get out of here."

Kayli returned the smile and ran her fingers through her
hair.

"And check your hair."

Kayli laughed and pulled her purse out of a drawer.
Ready or not, she was headed out to a second pretend date.

She paused at the building door, and took in the sight of
Shawn on a marble bench, waiting for her with his ankle
across his knee. The dark blue dress pants and light blue

button down shirt gave him a professional look.

Two women came up the walk to the building, and both stared at him. His eyes remained on the door. She waited until the women passed her, then stepped out. He bounded up and met her halfway and took her hand.

The smile he gave her made her heart race. It reminded her of the early days with Max. Kayli smiled back and the tight knot in her stomach melted away. He dropped an almost brotherly kiss on her forehead and stepped back. "Now, let's get some food."

The food cart occupied a parking space in front of her building, not always the same space. They each ordered a sandwich from the list on the whiteboard, bag of chips and a drink. The vendor bagged their selection and handed it to Shawn.

"You lunch together now? Before I only see you separate," the man said.

Shawn put an arm around Kayli. "We met when we each got food here."

The man beamed and clasped his hands. "That's wonderful!"

Shawn and Kayli waved, strolled to the corner and crossed the street to the park.

"Sun or shade?" Shawn asked.

"Sun. I'm indoors all day at work, and my windows face north. I need all the sunshine I can get."

"Sun it is." Shawn steered her down the angled walk that led to the center of the park. He chose a bench on the other side of a fountain, sat, and patted the seat beside him. She sat, but not too close. They faced the fountain and one of the streets.

Shawn slid closer as he handed Kayli her drink and a straw. His thigh barely grazed hers, but the warmth spread to places she didn't want to think about. She opened her drink, popped in the straw, and took a swallow before setting it on the bench on her other side.

He set his soda down, and reached back into the bag. Their fingers brushed when she took her sandwich. She couldn't tell if he was intentionally touching her. They were supposed to be pretending. He didn't need to do that.

"How are you doing?" Shawn asked.

"I'm a little nervous. Do you think he's watching?" Her gaze darted around without turning her head.

"I've got it covered. You can relax and eat. I can see the sidewalks along both streets and the walk leading here. We're supposed to be getting to know each other." He peeled open the wrapper on his sandwich.

"Okay." Max had always been the one to protect her. He'd bought the security system for the house for those times he had to work late. When they'd walked, he always moved between her and anything he considered a threat. Now she had to put her trust in a man she'd met only a few days ago, but it wasn't as hard as she expected. He'd put himself between her and danger, just as Max had.

Kayli opened her sandwich wrapper. "What's your boss's name?" If he was supposed to be Shawn Williams, she should learn more about that cover.

His grinned. "Adam. He's got all kinds of projects for me. Apparently, I haven't been in the office too much recently." Shawn took a drink of his soda, and set the can on the bench.

Kayli's eyes darted to Shawn's face and away. She put her can down. "I'd love to talk to Michael soon. I've never been separated from him for more than one night. I'm worried about how he's coping. He doesn't know Jackie as well as Michelle, and he didn't get to take his favorite stuffed animal or any of his clothes."

Shawn touched the hand Kayli had resting in her lap.

47

"I'm sorry the two of you have to go through this. How about if we set up a Skype call in my—well, my brother's office? If this guy is tracking your phone, he won't find out, and it'll look like you're visiting me at work."

Kayli gave him a smile. "Thank you."

A man jogged up and sat on the far side of the fountain. Kayli hissed in a breath.

"Don't look so worried," Shawn whispered. "Look at him out of the corner of your eye. Does he look familiar?"

She kept her gaze on two women coming up the path. They chattered, and ignored everything around them. The guy at the fountain seemed to watch the women and turned to follow their movements after they passed. He hadn't noticed her. A few minutes later, another man stopped beside him and they jogged off together.

She huffed out a breath. A false alarm.

Shawn tipped his drink up to his mouth and swallowed, then returned the can to the bench. "He's unlikely to be the one, but was he familiar?"

"No, not at all." That man was gone, and had barely looked their way, but someone was watching. She could feel it.

"Okay. So, let's continue with this date," Shawn said. "We need to look like we're having an enjoyable conversation, so let me tell you about my brothers. Since I'm the oldest, and the most responsible, my brothers used to tell me I was bossy. Okay. So, sometimes they still do. But, I was only bossy when I tried to keep them from getting into trouble. Like the time when Adam was nine and he broke his arm. I'd been going with my friends to a bike park with ramps for doing bike jumps. For a couple weeks, we'd been working our way from the easy jumps to the harder ones. We'd finally decided we were ready for the most awesome jump."

She smiled at the glow in his eyes. "I can picture you doing those jumps over and over."

"The big one ramped up to fifteen feet high, then you dropped onto a lower ramp on the other side of a gap. All three of us had done it, and we're high-fiving each other when Adam rides up. He says he's going to do it, too. I tried to stop him. I explained to him how we started on the little jumps. He looked at those jumps and said they were for babies. He rode back a distance and started the run. I stepped in front of the ramp, but he went around me. Sometimes I wonder if he'd have made it if I hadn't done that. Going up the ramp, he slowed a bit at the top. He sailed over and came short. The rear wheel was too low and hit the front of the ramp, sending Adam flying over the handlebars. And he broke his arm. He was lucky he didn't do anything else."

Even as a child, Shawn tried to be a protector. Then he found a job where he could protect other people, too.

"I'm sorry," he said. "I was supposed to tell you a funny story, and now I've made you sad."

"It's okay. I see how much you care for your brothers. I was a lonely only child until Michelle's family moved in next door when I was eleven. She has a sister and three brothers. I spent as much time with them as at my house." She smiled at the remembered antics. "We rode our bikes, too. Our moms let us go to the public pool by ourselves, and we rode our bikes to the theater. We did sleepovers. Sometimes we followed Michelle's older brother, Tommy, and his friends around. They were two years older than us. There was this steep hill in the woods the guys raced down. Michelle and I secretly practiced that hill, taking it slow at first. Eventually, we were ready to show the boys what we could do." She laughed. "I don't know how we never broke any bones."

Shawn grinned. "So, you're a daredevil, too?"

"I think that was the only really daring thing I did. Don't

ask me to do it now. I think I'd be more scared than the first time I saw that hill."

The memories were a reminder of what Michael was missing. "I never wanted to have an only child. Max and I planned on more children. At least Michael gets to play with Michelle's daughter, Kim, every weekday. Well, he did." So much for having a fun fake date. Her thoughts kept straying to sad memories.

Shawn shifted and his leg brushed hers. An accident or a distraction? "And he will again. We'll take care of this as fast as we can."

She liked his touch. And she shouldn't. Shawn had practice at pretending, and she had to remember that's all it was.

He checked his watch. "Lunch time's over. Nobody looked suspicious, but there were several lone guys who passed. We don't know if we're being observed, but just in case."

Shawn put his thumb and forefinger under Kayli's chin and turned her head toward him. His kiss was too short. It had been so long since she felt anything like this. She didn't want it to end, and leaned in, touched her lips to his again. He put his hand behind her head and deepened the kiss.

After a minute, Shawn put his forehead against hers. "I'm sorry. I shouldn't have done that," he whispered.

Kayli reared back. "Oh, my God!" She dropped her elbows to her legs, leaned forward and buried her face in her hands. He had stopped with one little show kiss. She was the one who couldn't get enough. Her libido had decided to wake up now, when affection between them was supposed to be an act.

Kayli straightened and pulled in a breath. She stared at a mother pushing a stroller on the other side of the fountain. "It was my fault. You were pulling away." She looked at him then turned away again. She closed her eyes and took several slow, deep breaths, and finally her normal calm returned.

Shawn stood and held his hand out. "It's all right. Let me walk you to your building."

They walked to the edge of the park and crossed the street. To the side of the door at Kayli's building, he closed in and repeated the almost kiss from the other night. He whispered in her ear. "Just to make sure."

Maybe that's what he'd tried to do at the park and she'd made it a real kiss.

Because she hadn't moved, he nudged her toward the door. She wondered if he'd kissed her in the park because he couldn't resist or if being so much in the open, he had to kiss her for real. She hoped it was because he couldn't help himself.

Chapter 9

Kayli's first waking thought was of Michael. Shawn had called the night before to let her know he'd arranged for her to talk to her son. He would pick her up and they'd go to his brother's office for the Skype call to Jackie that afternoon. To see her son's little face and talk to him, lifted her spirits more than anything had in the last few weeks.

She picked up her purse and computer bag from the coffee table and headed out the door. The car beeped and unlocked at a push of the button. As she reached for the door handle, she froze.

Another one. Her gaze fastened on the envelope on her windshield with her name scrawled across it in large curly letters. Just like the last one.

Her purse and bag slipped from her lifeless fingers and dropped on her feet. She barely felt the hit. Fear prevented her from touching the letter. Tears formed in her eyes, but she blinked them back.

Kayli squatted beside her purse, pulled out her cell phone, and dialed Shawn's number. Please, please be close to your phone. She stood and stared at the envelope again.

He answered on the first ring. "Hi, Kayli. I—"

"Shawn." She put every fear she had in that one word.

"Kayli, what's wrong?" His words burst through the line.

She held the phone like a lifeline, but he wouldn't be able to reel her in.

"Answer me! Are you all right?"

A deep breath steadied her. "There's another one." She'd said it. She willed the envelope to disappear, but it remained, taunting her. It represented pain and suffering and death.

"Another—letter?" Shawn's voice soothed, probably so she wouldn't panic.

"Yes." Kayli drew in another breath. "I don't know what to do. I'm afraid to touch it. I'm afraid to find out what it says."

"Don't touch it. I want you to go back into the house and turn on your alarm. I'll call Al and meet him there ASAP."

"Okay." She wouldn't have to look at it while she waited. She'd have trouble *not* thinking about it, though.

"Don't hang up until you're secured inside." His voice had grown tense.

Quick steps took her to the door. She fumbled with the key, but made it inside, twisting both locks and then setting the alarm. "I'm in."

"Good. I'll see you soon."

She couldn't sit. Too much jumpy energy flowed through her nerves. Every few minutes she peeked out the window. Finally, a cruiser pulled up and a uniformed officer stepped out. She opened her door and stared out.

The officer put his hand up. "Don't touch the car, ma'am."

"I don't want anywhere near that thing." She wrapped her arms around herself. The policeman seemed to be standing guard.

A few minutes later, Shawn parked on the street and sprinted up to her. Al wasn't far behind.

Al pulled on latex gloves before he slit the envelope open, and extracted the folded sheet of paper. Touching it as little as possible, he unfolded it on the hood of the car. "Now, let's see what we've got here."

Shawn leaned in and read, then glanced at Kayli.

She shook her head. "I don't want to know."

"No direct threats," Shawn said. "He seems educated."

She glanced at the page and back to Shawn. "How can you tell in only three lines?"

"Correct use of contractions and no misspelling. You should see some of the letters from kidnappers that I've come across." Shawn straightened up. "I think you should read it. You need to know everything you're up against."

She stared at Shawn and Al. Shawn stared back, waiting for her response. Her breaths came too fast and she worked at slowing them down. She didn't want to know, but he was right. Anything could be the key to finding out who this was. "All right!"

She stepped up between them, and Shawn touched her arm. "Don't touch it."

He seriously thought she'd touch it? She read the four sentences.

I know your kid's alive. If he comes back, you'll wish he hadn't.

Now get rid of the new boyfriend or you'll wish you had.

Your love belongs to me.

She laced her hands together, but that didn't stop their trembling. She glared at Shawn. "Well, you got your wish. Now he's going after you. Please be careful."

"I always am."

Her gaze strayed back to the letter. She didn't want to see it again, but something struck her. "That last sentence...Its—"

"He wants you to love only him, so he's taking away anyone else you love."

"If I'm supposed to fall in love with him, doesn't that mean I know him already?" Kayli was vaguely aware that Al stood back and watched them. "Someone I know is a killer." She could have stood next to him, talked to him.

"Most likely. Or he was ready to make a move on you and I got in the way."

Al folded up the letter. "Let's get this put away." He slid it and the envelope into a plastic bag. "I'll check it for prints, and let you know if we find anything."

Al and the officer left and Shawn touched Kayli's arm. "I'll follow you to your office. To explain being late, you can tell your secretary that I called this morning and you lost track of time. I'll come around four to take you to the Skype call with Michael. Don't tell anyone you're going to talk to him. We don't want it to get back to this guy that you have any contact with your son."

The chill came back. Shawn must have seen it because he put his hand over hers. "I'll see you later."

It was a comfort, seeing his car behind hers.

Chapter 10

Late afternoon took forever to come. Until Kayli laid eyes on Shawn again, she worried about him. How long would the killer give her to get rid of Shawn before he did it his way? Shawn had more experience protecting himself than Max had, but Shawn could still be taken by surprise.

Shawn arrived. She'd already put away her work, so she jointed him in the outer office. He gave her a kiss on the cheek and took her hand. All show for Monica.

She introduced them, and Monica squinted at him. Probably trying to figure out if he was good enough for Kayli.

"Bye, Monica. I'll see you tomorrow."

"We have to see Al first," Shawn said after they reached the elevator. He led Kayli to his car. He seemed more tense than when he'd faced the prospect of being the killer's target.

"What's wrong? Did something else happen?"

He stopped beside his car and squeezed her shoulder. "We'll discuss it at the police station."

Shawn didn't speak again until they entered Al's office. "Let me see the print pattern."

Al showed him a paper.

"That's it? That's the only print on the page? It doesn't even make sense. How could she fold the paper?"

Al must have told Shawn something on the phone. Shawn seemed to understand what he was going to see.

"She could have worn gloves," Al said.

Shawn dropped the page on the desk. "Wore gloves to

fold it, but not to pick it up? Someone wants it to look like she's behind it."

Kayli's eyes darted from one man to the other. "Are you talking about me?"

Shawn ran a hand through his hair. "Sorry. I should have come here before picking you up."

"You *are* talking about me?"

Shawn glared at Al.

Al pointed to a chair in front of his desk. "Have a seat, Kayli." Shawn sat down beside her. She studied his face. This was going to be bad.

She steeled herself for the news, and looked at Al. "What is it?"

"Kayli, we ran the prints on the note from this morning. The envelope's clean except for a smudged partial on a corner. The paper however has four clear fingerprints. They're yours."

"What? You're the only one who touched it."

Al leaned forward. "Which means you touched the paper before it went into the envelope."

"I didn't. I never saw it before you took it out. This makes no sense. How is that possible?" She gave Shawn a worried look.

"I don't know. We'll figure it out." He stood. "Let's go to my office."

After they were back in Shawn's car, she felt able to talk. "Does Al think I wrote those letters?"

He glanced at her and away, starting the car. "He thinks it's a possibility."

"It makes no sense! If I'd killed Max—" She blinked, but it didn't hold back the tears. "I'd already gotten away with it and I wouldn't bring attention to it again." She swiped at the tears on her cheeks. "I wouldn't have hired you. You know I didn't do it, right?"

He took her hand. "Kayli, I know how much you love your son. You wouldn't do this. I know how hard it's been for you to get over Max's death, so I know you couldn't have been involved in that either. As a police officer, Al's got to look at every angle. I doubt he believes it either, but he found out you have a life insurance policy on Michael, and that didn't sit well with him."

She tipped her head back and let her breath out. "Yes, there is an insurance policy on Michael. Max was an insurance agent, and he set it up about a week after Michael was born."

"Fifty-thousand dollars?"

"I don't know. I never saw the paperwork. There was one on Max, too. I got seven-hundred-fifty-thousand dollars when he died. I paid off the house and took a six month leave because I was scared of something happening to Michael. I haven't touched any of the money since." She'd totally forgotten about the policy on Michael. It was paid directly out of the insurance proceeds she'd received. Even if she had thought of it, it wouldn't have seemed relevant to her.

"And you?"

"Max was an insurance agent. Of course, there's one on me. It's for three-hundred-thousand."

"This sheds a whole new light on your situation."

A chill went down her spine. It could be about money. Why did that seem worse than it being about her? "Why?"

"Let me think about it for a bit before we discuss it." He put the car in gear and pulled into the street.

She didn't like that answer. "I want to discuss it now. How would someone know I collected insurance money? The only person I told was Michelle. And I haven't changed how I live." Except the only person she shared her life with now was her son.

"I want to check some things out first. We'll discuss it

later."

As they entered Adam's office building, Kayli pushed away all those horrible thoughts, and focused on Michael. Soon, she'd see her baby's face and talk to him. It was bittersweet. See him and not touch him. They'd have to say good-bye again, but she would cherish every moment they had.

Shawn introduced Kayli to the receptionist, Casey, who teased him about Kayli being the first woman he'd brought to the office.

He hurried her into his office and shut the door. "I hope they're not too upset that we're late."

He pulled a second chair behind the desk and invited her to sit. His fingers flew across the keys as he made the connection.

"Mommy!" Michael's hand reached for the screen.

He probably thought he could touch her. It was the first time he'd seen anyone like this. She reached for the screen. "I miss you, honey."

"Me, too, Mommy. Dom is fun." At least Jackie's son helped take his mind off being away from her and home.

"I have a new friend." said Kayli. Shawn waved. "His name is Shawn."

"Hi, Michael. It's nice to meet you."

Michael's eyes shifted to his left for a few seconds. "Mommy, I want to come home."

Kayli's heart clenched at his sad little voice. Shawn squeezed her hand. She wasn't totally alone in this. "It's not safe yet, honey. Let's talk about what we want to do when you get back home." She wished she could go there right now, scoop him up and take him home.

He bounced in his seat. "Can Kim come have a sleep over?"

"Yes, of course she can. We'll have to plan something

special for the two of you to do when she comes."

They made plans for a few more minutes. "What have you been doing with Dom?"

"Boy stuff." He spent many more minutes telling Kayli about the fun he was having with Dom. The type of stories that she'd hug him over as she laughed.

"Mommy. I'm going to preschool with Dom."

"That sounds fun. Are you making new friends?"

"Yeah. We even had Jimmy come over after school."

"I bet that was fun." Michael had a whole life without her. She didn't know his new friends, and hadn't met their parents.

His eyes lit up. "Dom's dad took us fishing. I only caught little fish. Dom caught a big one that we had for dinner. I want to go fishing when I get home."

Fishing. She knew nothing about it. Max hadn't fished, either. Maybe one of Max's brothers fished. Her little boy was enjoying new experiences and she wasn't with him for them. It was as if he was that big boy he claimed to be. And she didn't like it.

Shawn nudged her and twirled a finger. It was too soon to wrap up. She'd missed so many conversations with Michael.

"Honey, I'm sure it's nearly dinner time there, and I'm getting hungry, too. It's time to say good-bye."

"No!"

Kayli blinked back tears. "I'm sorry. Remember that I love you." She kissed her finger and held it in front of the camera.

Michael calmed quickly. "Me, too." He kissed his finger and held it to the screen, so that it disappeared when it got close.

"I'll call you again in a few days."

Shawn shut down the connection.

She'd held her tears back for Michael's sake, but couldn't hold them anymore. Shawn plucked a tissue from the box on his desk and handed it to her.

"Thank you. It was hard, but it was worth it. Better than not having seen him." She missed her baby even more now, but reminded herself, just like she'd reminded Michael, that it wasn't safe yet.

"I know I can't call Michael from my cell, home or office phones, but what about doing skype calls from home? Who's going to know?"

He put his hands on her shoulders. "We don't know how tech savvy this guy is. He might have access to your computer and be able to intercept your calls."

She nodded, keeping her head down. For a few minutes, she thought she'd be able to talk to her son every night, read him bedtime stories. Dashed hopes made it harder.

"But, I'll run some tests on your computer and add some intercept software, to monitor it."

She sucked in a breath. "Does that mean we can do it?"

He shrugged. "No promises. Maybe."

One step closer.

Shawn wrapped an arm around her shoulder. "I'll drive you back to your car and then follow you home." She nodded and they walked out the door.

They stepped into the waning sunlight and Kayli lifted her face up. "I want this all to be over."

Shawn squeezed her hand. "We're getting somewhere. He's going to slip up."

Neither talked on the few blocks to Kayli's car.

Shawn pulled into the nearly empty lot, and grabbed her hand. "I'll stay back a ways and see if anyone follows you."

She bit her bottom lip.

"Are you all right to drive home?"

"Yes, but it would be nice to forget that someone's

probably watching."

"I'm watching."

She almost smiled. "But I like *your* eyes." She turned away and climbed into her car.

~~~

"I'll see you soon." He watched her leave. No one followed. He didn't expect it. They'd only been in the parking lot for a minute and hadn't been followed from the office.

He rolled to the exit. A silver Accord pulled in behind Kayli, and Black Mercedes dropped in behind it from a street parking space. He waited for another car and pulled in behind.

After several blocks, Kayli went straight through an intersection, and the two cars behind her turned left. Shawn made note of the license plates anyway. The Cooper directly in front of him, turned off a few blocks from Kayli's house.

He pulled into her driveway, parked beside her and got out. He looked around the neighborhood. The previous time he'd been there, it had been dark. It was upscale, but not too expensive. No vehicles were parked on the street.

Kayli opened her door and walked in. Shawn looked around then followed her to her security panel. "I'm going to canvas the neighborhood to see if anyone saw a stranger in the area during the night or early morning and then I'll check over your security system to make sure it's good."

She frowned. "Will they talk to you?"

"I'll tell them I'm a friend of yours and you saw someone lurking around your car."

A half-hour later, he entered the house to the scent of cooking beef and tomato sauce. He joined Kayli in the kitchen.

"Did you find out anything?"

He shook his head. "Nobody I talked to saw anything."

Shawn pointed into the other room. "Now, I'll check out your security system."

"While you do that, I'll finish making dinner." She turned back to the stove and flipped browned steaks that were simmering in tomato sauce and vegetables.

"You didn't have to do that."

She glanced over her shoulder. "I've been making dinner for one for a couple of weeks. It's nice to make dinner for two."

She quickly turned away and Shaw wasn't sure if he'd seen another tear. He couldn't imagine how difficult it would be to have a young son living with someone else and being so concerned about his safety.

Shawn faced the security panel and pulled out his phone. He dialed the number on the panel. "Hi. This is Shawn Gordon. Is Jeff Andrews in?" He waited. "Hey, Jeff. How's married life?"

"Hey, Shawn. It's good."

They chatted for a few more minutes before Shawn got to the point. "Can you check one of your systems? Kayli McAllister." He gave the address.

"Got it up. What do you need?"

"I want to find out when the system was installed and if there are improvements that can be made."

Shawn listened to Jeff click. "Max McAllister. Five years."

"Has it been tested since then?"

"Nope. Nothing since it was installed."

"I want to set up an appointment. Check the system out. Install outdoor cameras, especially one that points at the driveway. Upgrade anything that needs it. Check locks, and upgrade them if they need it, too."

"I'll do it personally. How about day after tomorrow?"

"Okay. I'll be here. Thanks, Jeff."

Shawn walked into the kitchen. "I have the security company coming to check out your system and install cameras. Maybe we'll catch this guy if he leaves another message."

Kayli frowned. "Do you think the guy will notice the new cameras? He avoided them at the playground."

"Hopefully, not right away. At the very least, we'll find out about what time he comes."

Maybe the next time, they'd see his face, and Kayli would recognize him.

"We're going to get through this. We'll find out who this is." Shawn lifted his nose in the air. "By the way, that smells delicious."

"Swiss steak." She checked the stove timer. "It should be ready in ten minutes. Do you want to set the table?"

"Sure." She hadn't come out and asked him to join her for dinner, but he'd take it. She was starting to slip into more-than-a-client territory.

"Plates. Silverware. Glasses." She pointed to a different cupboard with each word.

Very soon they were seated across from each other enjoying the food and conversation.

"You're a wonderful cook, Kayli. I'll have to show off one of my culinary specialties, too." He wouldn't mind staring at her face every night during dinner. He'd enjoy working on a meal together.

She rested her chin on her hand. "You can cook?"

Shawn smiled. "My mom made sure all four of us could cook. I think she did it so she wouldn't have to as often." He smiled and Kayli laughed.

"So what was her specialty?"

"Stuffed peppers."

"I love stuffed peppers. Can you make them, too?"

"Of course. How about if I make them while I'm here with the security company?"

Kayli frowned. "Okay."

"What's wrong?" Shawn asked.

"Well, I have to work, but I can give you a key."

"And the code to the security system. Or I'll wait outside until the security guy gets here and he can disarm it."

"Oh, um. Okay." She rattled off the code.

Shawn sat back and laced his fingers over his stomach. It had been as good as, if not better than any meal his mother made. Not something he'd tell her. "Thanks." He stood and picked up his plate and glass. "Let me help you with dishes and then I'll leave."

She shook her head.

"What? You don't want my help with dishes?"

"Oh, just crazy things going through my head. Thanks for the help." She smiled and stood, too.

He wondered what crazy things she'd been thinking, and hoped they involved getting to know him better. She seemed more comfortable with him, which was good. Really good, because he wanted to kiss her again. For them, and not anyone else.

After putting his dishes in the dishwasher, he started scrubbing pans. He could feel her watching him, and wondered if she liked what she saw.

"I'll go get the key." Her voice was low and sexy. Maybe she *had* liked the view.

She returned as Shawn was drying his hands, and held the key out to him. He wrapped his hand around her hand as well as the key. He watched her eyes. He so much wanted to kiss her, but it wouldn't be professional and she wasn't ready for it. At least, there was no fear in her eyes this time. Maybe... No.

Control. He needed to remember he was working for Kayli, and not her boyfriend. Move away from her. He took the key from her hand, stepped back, and inhaled a couple of times before he could speak. "Walk me to the door. I do have to leave."

Shawn took her hand and pulled her to the door. "Stuffed peppers in two days," he whispered and didn't kiss her like he wanted to.

She studied his face before closing the door. He couldn't read what she was thinking. The lock clicked.

This was turning into so much more than play acting. There was no pretending. He was falling for her. If only Kayli was ready for it.

Chapter 11

Two days later after work, Kayli pulled into her driveway beside Shawn's car, and got out, noticing the new camera attached to the corner of the garage eaves. Her first thought was that maybe they'd see the killer's face, but then she realized that if he saw the camera, he'd be unlikely to attack her in the driveway. It already made her feel safer. Rounding the garage, she saw another camera over the door. She stopped and spun around. Were there other cameras that she couldn't see?

Inside the house, a surge of happiness overtook her when she thought of Shawn waiting for her. She pushed down the emotion. He was being paid to protect her and find the killer so Michael could come home. This was just another job to him.

The delicious smell of peppers and seasoned tomato sauce caused her stomach to growl, and pulled her to the kitchen. "A chef's hat?" She covered her mouth. Over his jeans and t-shirt, he wore her apron that was covered in puppies that Michelle had helped Michael get her for Christmas. He was more delicious than she had a right to notice.

He pouted. "What? You don't think I'm a chef? Doesn't this food smell fantastic?"

She tried not to smile. "It smells wonderful. But isn't the hat a bit much?"

Shawn grinned, pulled the hat off and tossed it on the counter. "It got the response I was hoping for, so it was *not* a bit much."

"Thanks. I'm going to change and then I'll set the table."

A few minutes later Kayli came back to the kitchen bare foot, wearing jeans and a t-shirt. She set plates and silverware on the table kitty-corner to each other, and went back to the kitchen, as Shawn pulled a pan out of the oven.

Her stomach growled. "Red and green ones. I've never had stuffed red peppers."

He glanced at her. "You'll love them." He reached into the oven and pulled out another pan, six perfectly baked corn muffins. He popped the muffins out one at a time and put them into a paper towel lined bowl.

"I brought red wine, if you want to get glasses." He loaded their plates with one of each color pepper, and set the remaining ones on the table. Then he retrieved the muffins and wine from the kitchen, opened the wine and poured, then seated himself. He took a sip of wine, but didn't start to eat.

Kayli cut out a chunk of red pepper, loaded her fork and slid it in her mouth. "Mmm. It tastes as good as it smells. You are a superb chef, sir."

Shawn smiled and tipped his head. "Thank you, ma'am." He split and buttered a muffin.

He had a five o'clock shadow she wished she was bold enough to touch. The previous evenings, he must have shaved before she saw him. She used to enjoy running her fingers up and down Max's stubbly jaw, and wondered if Shawn's would feel the same.

"I have another story about my brothers."

She tipped her head. "What about a story about you?"

One corner of his mouth tipped up. "My brothers have funnier stories."

"I'm sure that's not what they think."

"Maybe." He stared at the ceiling. "Okay. Here's one. In high school, I tended to get into trouble."

She frowned. Before, he'd told her he was very responsible.

He held up a finger. "I did not get into fights, and I almost never skipped classes. But I did do practical jokes. My classmates loved them, but not so much the teachers and staff. Or my parents."

"I was the strait-laced kid who tried to do everything right." They were so different, but maybe opposites attracted.

"One day, I walked into Miss Jordan's English Lit class, with a cup of coffee and set it on her desk. You could smell the vanilla flavored creamer, just like she liked it. She wasn't in yet, so I set it on her desk, and an upside-down cup, then took my seat. She asked who brought the coffee when she came in, but nobody would tell her. Everybody knew I had something planned, but they didn't know what yet."

"She wouldn't drink coffee that was just sitting there?" she asked.

"Of course not. That wasn't what it was for." His lip twitched, and Kayli was sure he was trying not to smile. "She put a stack of papers on her desk, sat down and picked up her attendance sheet. Once she finished with that, she noticed the upside-down cup. Every eye in the room stared at that cup. Miss Jordan didn't look like she wanted to lift it, but finally gave in."

Kayli leaned forward. "What was under it?"

Shawn leaned forward and whispered. "A spider."

She gasped and smacked against the back of the chair. "No! That would have scared me half to death."

Shawn smiled. "She screamed, knocked over the coffee and jumped away from the desk. I ran up and killed the spider and disposed of it."

"How big was it?"

"About the size of a nickel."

"Why did you do that to her?" It seemed really mean,

and not at all like the man she was beginning to know.

"I didn't want to take the test that day. It was the test papers that she'd set on her desk, and now they were soaking in spilled coffee. Unusable."

She bit her lip to hold back a smile. She sure hoped Michael didn't do things like that. "So, what happened?"

"She knew it was me. I got sent to the office for the rest of the period. The next day, we had the test and my copy had ten extra questions, which I aced." He beamed.

"So you could have taken the test that day."

He grinned. "No. I'd gone out the night before and hadn't studied. That night, I studied like crazy."

"What did your parents say?"

Another grin. "Dad thought it was hilarious, but not Mom. I was grounded for a week. If I wasn't eating or sleeping, I had to be doing homework or reading a book."

"That seems fair."

"I didn't think so at the time, but it *was* fair. I hope I'll be as good a parent as they are."

"So, your mom was the tough parent?"

"Hell, no. Sometimes Dad was much harsher than that, and Mom was the softy. It just depended on what we did. If it was something that involved our safety, dad came down really hard, and Mom was just glad we were okay."

"I worry about being a single parent. Right now, it's fine. But, as Michael gets older, I don't have the father perspective on things. Max was so excited about being a father and had all kinds of things he'd planned on doing with Michael when he got older." She blinked at the tears that had sprung up. "Michael's going to miss out on so much."

Shawn's hand covered her arm. It was just meant to reassure, but a tingle arrowed into her chest.

"I'm sure Michelle's husband could offer advice."

"And Donny has already, but it's not the same." She

wished she hadn't turned Shawn's story into something that made her sad.

He laced his fingers on top of his head. "Okay. Let me tell you a story about something my parents didn't find out about."

Before long, Shawn teased laughter from her. It felt good, but there was still the underlying sadness of missing Michael and Max.

Before she knew it, she'd finished her food. "I can't believe I ate three halves."

"I'm glad you liked it. Now, you load the dishwasher and I'll wash the pans." He picked up his dishes and carried them to the kitchen.

She finished first and leaned against the counter as he dried the baking pan. Even washing dishes, he looked way sexier than she should notice. He finished and caught her staring at him. Again that corner of his mouth tipped up. Yeah. Way too sexy.

"Now I'll show you the improvements to your security system." Shawn led her to the security panel. "It's a new panel. There are three screens on it; one for each camera."

"I saw two out front. Where's the third?" Kayli asked.

"It's outside your sliding doors in back. There's a hard drive behind the panel that will record the video. It's also sent at the end of each day to the security company. You can review each camera individually." He showed her the video of her arriving home. "Jeff also checked all the windows and doors. Two of the windows had defective wiring. One upstairs, one downstairs. The locks are good."

"I feel safer already. Thank you, Shawn."

"I want you to be safe."

That look. Like he really wanted to be with her, and she wasn't just a client. Her heart kicked into a faster pace. He was the first man she'd even thought of spending time with since...Max.

"Should I leave?"

"Stay."

He reached up and dropped his hand down. Maybe he wanted to touch her and changed his mind. Maybe he was nervous, or thought she was. "Okay. You go sit, and I'll get the wine."

Shawn joined her in the living room with the half finished bottle and two glasses. He handed her one and sat so close, their legs and shoulders touched.

Kayli sipped her wine and thought how nice it felt sitting beside him. His warmth along her side filled her body with a longing that she'd been missing for too long. Snuggled next to Max had been comfortable. Beside Shawn, it was different, but still nice.

She took another sip. Maybe the wine gave her some warmth, relaxed her. "When we went on our first fake date, I wasn't ready. I had to tell myself that it was for show to get Michael back home." She studied Shawn's face. "After the initial awkwardness, I enjoyed myself." She turned forward again. "I think I'm ready to really date again...mostly." Guilt still tore a hole in her gut. Hopefully, more time would ease that.

"So, it doesn't matter what guy you date?" Shawn asked.

Her stomach seemed to flip over and she tightened her mouth. He was the reason she felt able to date again, and he knew it.

Shawn kissed her temple. "If I helped in any way with that, I'm glad."

He took her hand in his warmer one, and lifted it to his lips, kissing her fingers, then lowered their hands to his thigh.

She sipped the wine and leaned against Shawn, then lifted her feet onto the coffee table. He kicked his shoes off and followed suit, then drained his glass and took hers, setting them on the table beside him.

After a few minutes, he lifted Kayli's legs, swinging them over his own. He rubbed a hand down her shin before pulling her knees to his chest. Not the sexiest move, but, boy, did that speed up her heart rate. Excitement and panic hit at the same time. It was probably her imagination that she could feel his heart beating against her leg.

He rubbed his hand gently up and down her back, and soon she relaxed. He slid her onto his lap, one arm behind her back, the other hand at her hip. He watched her as he drew closer, maybe giving her time to stop him. She almost did. Fear of opening up again fought with the need to feel a man's touch.

He gave her a gentle kiss. This kiss wasn't for someone else's eyes. She pulled back and examined his face. Interest, not passion. But she wouldn't have been able to deal with passion, not yet. She hadn't been this physically close to a man since Max. The whole evening was a bittersweet memory, but different.

Max didn't cook, but occasionally he'd left work early and picked up one of her favorite meals. The table would be set and food warming in the oven until she arrived home. They'd have pleasant conversation, and over a chocolaty dessert…they didn't always finish dessert.

She lowered her head to Shawn's shoulder and he tightened his hold on her, rubbing his hand up and down her back. Maybe passion did simmer below the surface. She'd given three years to loneliness, and didn't want to give it any more of her life.

After a minute he kissed her forehead. "Are you okay?"

Kayli laced her fingers through his. "Mmmm." She kissed his neck.

Chapter 12

Kayli caught herself smiling again as she rested her chin on her hand as she sat at her office desk. That morning, she'd wakened on the couch, her pillow tucked under her head and a blanket over her. Before sitting up, she knew she was alone in the house. The wine and glasses were gone, and a note with her name scrawled on it stood like a pup tent on the coffee table.

Leave it to Shawn to ease her mind.

You looked so cute curled up on the couch, I didn't want to wake you when I left. I took the liberty of kissing your forehead. I'm going to reset the security system and keep the key you gave me so I can lock up.

Shawn

Monica walked into Kayli's office. "You look like the cat that swallowed the canary."

"No, the canary's still alive," Kayli responded.

"I don't think so."

"I just had the best night of sleep in weeks."

Monica gave her a disbelieving look. "Good sleep doesn't cause smiles like that. What happened before sleep?"

"You're right. I had dinner with Shawn. We had wine and I fell asleep on the couch. Then he left. What you're thinking, didn't happen."

Monica's eyes widened. "That's it? I wouldn't be smiling over that."

"He *did* leave a really sweet note," Kayli added.

"Oh, *that* explains it." Monica shook her head. "Enough

about your teenage romance. The reason I came in here was to ask if you wanted to join John and me for lunch today."

Monica had asked her several times and today she'd probably be good company at lunch. "All right. Is your brother coming up or are we meeting him somewhere?"

Monica eyes widened. "Really?" She smiled. "We'll meet him at *The Ranch*."

"Oh, I haven't eaten there yet. I've wanted to try it."

"It's really good. You won't be disappointed," Monica said.

An hour later they walked the four blocks to the restaurant.

At the restaurant, Monica paused with her hand on the door. "If I can't resist dessert, we'll have to take the long way back."

Kayli laughed. "I'll split dessert with you and we can walk back through the park."

"It's a deal!"

"Are you two plotting?" asked a voice behind them.

They spun around.

"John!" Monica hugged her brother.

Kayli greeted him less exuberantly. "Hi, John. I hope you don't mind that Monica asked me to join you."

"You're always welcome, Kayli." He gave her a blinding smile. Inside the restaurant, they passed a life-size painted plastic statue of a steer before reaching the hostess. John gave his name and said there were three. They followed the hostess between solid oak tables to window seats. The women sat on one side of the table with John on the other. Small shelves on the walls and over the windows held worn cowboy boots with spurs, leather work gloves, and cowboy hats. Saddles hung over rails, separating the dining room from the bar. Large photographs of round-ups, some black and white, some color, decorated the walls. Country music played in the background, loud enough to hear, but not so loud to drown out the buzz of conversation.

Kayli sipped her water. "So, John, what did you do in California besides work?"

"I did a lot of sightseeing, hiked in the mountains. I learned to surf."

"I think I'd drown if I tried surfing," Monica said.

Kayli enjoyed swimming, but only in calm seas. "That doesn't appeal to me either, but sightseeing and hiking are fun."

The waitress stopped at the table and took their drink orders. They opened their menus and discussed lunch options. The waitress returned with drinks, and they placed their requests.

"John, didn't you meet a girl in California worth staying there for?" Kayli asked.

"I dated, but California girls just aren't the same as girls here."

"Is there someone special here?"

"Maybe."

"John!" Monica said, "You didn't tell me you were dating anyone."

"I'm not yet. I'm working on it."

"Oh. Well, I can give you pointers," she teased her brother.

They all laughed and conversation turned to events happening in the area. The food arrived and conversation slowed as they tasted their meals.

Monica mentioned that *Concerts in the Park* would be starting soon. "I went to some of them last year." She looked at Kayli. "We should go. We could go to dinner right from work and then go to the park."

Kayli hadn't gone since Max had taken her. She felt ready to experience life again. "That could be fun. Let me know when and who's playing."

"That reminds me of one of the free park concerts I went to," John said. "It was a cover of The Backstreet Boys nineties songs. The guy portraying Brian was singing *Quit Playing Games* when he stepped too close to the front of the stage and fell off. You should have seen the startled look on his face."

Kayli gasped and covered her mouth.

"It was only a two foot drop and he landed on his feet. Only missed a couple of words, and kept on singing. The crowd went wild."

"I can imagine," Kayli said.

Dessert arrived, and they discussed local past concerts. Kayli checked her watch. "It's time to get back to work. Monica, are you ready for that walk through the park?"

"Yes, boss."

Monica and Kayli pulled cash from their purses.

"No. Put that away. I'm paying." John slipped his wallet from his pocket, and fished out a credit card. "Go on, now. I'll wait for this."

They thanked him, and Monica gave him a hug.

"John, it was so nice to see you again," Kayli said.

John took her hand. "We'll have to do it again sometime."

He had such an earnest expression, like he was trying to figure her out. She tugged her hand away after he'd held it too long.

Kayli and Monica headed to the park. Monica droned on while Kayli thought about lunch. Maybe John was the one. He was recently back in town, so the timing was right. John used to stop by to see Monica once in a while, so they knew each other. He seemed pretty happy that she might join them at the concert. But, he was Monica's brother. There was no way he was crazy like that.

~~~

Later in the afternoon, Kayli's cell phone rang. Shawn's name flashed on the screen. She answered, smiling. "Thank you."

"Oh...yeah. You're welcome. You were okay this morning?"

"Wonderful. Thank you for the best night's sleep I've had in weeks."

"That was probably just the wine," Shawn responded.

"No, I've tried that and it didn't work." She lowered her voice a little. "It's all you."

"Um, thanks. Now I'm going to spoil it. When did you last add paper to your printer?"

Kayli automatically glanced at the printer. "Two or three weeks ago? That's a really strange question, Shawn."

"How about at home?"

"Probably two or three months. I don't print there very often. What's this about?"

"I'm on my way over. Don't print anything before I get there."

"But—" The phone had already gone silent. Kayli shrugged and set it down. She glanced back at the printer. Shawn had asked about the paper. What was important about that? She gasped and covered her mouth. The notes. Maybe the killer had gotten his paper from here. But, the whole company used the same paper, probably half the city, too. But, not all the paper had her prints on it.

She picked up her pen and threw it down. No way could she concentrate now. She got up and paced, stopped to stare out the window. Paced again. She checked the time. He should have been here by now. Anything could have delayed him. A phone call just as he was leaving, a new client stopping in, someone on the street needing help. Back at the window, she wished it looked out over the entrance. The later his arrival, the more dread built in her chest. Kayli stared at her desk clock, again. Shawn could have gotten there three times since his call.

Voices in the outer office brought her out of her thoughts. Shawn walked in and closed the door. She startled at his ripped shirt, dirty jeans and scraped forearm and knuckles. Her heart sped up and her hands shook so much, she clenched them together.

"Do you have a couple of large envelopes?" he asked.

"Envelopes? Shawn what happened to you?" There was no way she could ignore how he looked. She eyed each scrape, bruise and tear again.

"I had a little run-in with a car, but I'm okay."

Kayli gasped, the blood drained from her head and she leaned on her desk, palms flat. "It was him, wasn't it?"

He hurried to her and wrapped an arm around her, steadying her. He didn't answer until she looked at his face. Maybe her color had returned.

"Probably, but I didn't get a good look. I *do* know it was a man."

"Shawn, you should sit down." She led him to a chair and he sat. She sank into the chair beside his. "Tell me what happened!"

"Kayli, I'm fine. I didn't need it, but the paramedics checked me out."

She didn't recognize her voice as panic took over. "There were paramedics! Start talking."

He sighed, and his eyes didn't leave her as he spoke. "I left Adam's office to walk here. I was crossing a street with the light when a car whipped around the corner and hit me."

Kayli gasped and squeezed Shawn's arm. "You could have been killed."

Shawn winced, and she immediately lifted her hands

away. "Oh, I'm so sorry!"

"It's okay, Kayli." He smiled and held out his uninjured hand. "Hold this one."

She grasped it, so much warmer than her cold hands.

"I heard the squeal of tires, and started to step back to the curb, so he barely clipped me with the corner of the bumper."

She touched his face. "It doesn't seem like barely to me."

"I've just got some bruises and scratches. I'll be fine in no time."

Kayli frowned. The killer would try again once he found out that Shawn was still alive. Maybe he wouldn't be as fortunate the next time. "Shawn." She drew out his name. He wasn't going to like this. "Maybe we should have a public breakup."

"No!"

His strong response startled her.

"First," he held up one finger. "You can't get Michael back until you know he'll be safe. Second," he held up another finger. "He's still out there and could harm somebody else. And third," another finger went up. "He may escalate to actually kidnapping you."

Her head swam. "I hadn't thought of that. I just thought he wanted to make me miserable."

"And then he'll come along to make you feel better."

Kayli shivered. The most important thing was to keep doing this for Michael. She had to trust that Shawn could take care of himself. "All right, I don't want to think about that right now. Tell me why you came."

"Sorry, it's all the same. I was adding paper to my printer, when I realized that I was holding it the same way your fingerprints are on the killer's note. I want to compare the bottom sheet of paper from this printer and the one at your house."

She couldn't believe what he implied. "Are you saying that the killer took paper from *my* printer to write his note?" She shivered, grabbed her upper arms and rubbed them.

"There's only one way to find out." Shawn pulled gloves out of his pocket and put them on. "Do you have two large envelopes?" Kayli pulled two nine by twelve envelopes from the cabinet the printer sat on, and handed them over. He plucked a pen out of the pencil cup and wrote 'office' on one and 'home' on the other. He opened the printer's paper drawer, and pulled out the whole stack of paper, then separated the bottom sheet from the others and slid it into its designated envelope.

"Now, with your permission, I'll get the bottom sheet from your home printer and have Al check them for prints."

"All right. Be careful."

He touched her cheek. "I always am." He kissed her nose and walked out the door.

She dropped into her chair and touched her nose. No audience again, and he kissed her. She didn't know if he was still trying to make her comfortable or if it actually meant something. And maybe she wanted it to.

Then she reeled in any emotion and thought about how Shawn could have been killed, just like Max. Only his being more aware saved him from serious injury. She still sat stiffly at her desk when Monica strolled in.

"What happened to him?"

"He got hit by a car." To her ears, her voice was under control. Inside, her body temperature must have dropped five degrees. A jacket wouldn't warm her.

"A car!" Monica's eyes widened in fear. "Oh, Kayli. And he came here directly from the scene?"

She nodded, not able to speak, reliving another accident.

"Why isn't he at the hospital?"

"He said the paramedics checked him out." She stared at

81

Monica, trying to concentrate on *her* face, and not the one in her head.

"He's one tough dude," Monica responded in admiration. "But you don't look so tough."

"He could have died," Kayli whispered. She couldn't keep up the calm pretense when images of a bloody Max wouldn't leave her head. Shawn had been injured by the same man who had killed Max.

Monica dragged a chair to Kayli's side and held her hand. "He didn't. He's not going to. You're shivering. I'll get you some—chamomile tea. We really need some alcohol here," she muttered as she went to the coffee station in her office. She was back within minutes, handing Kayli a cup and reseating herself. "Here. It's the best I can do."

"Thanks, Monica. I'll be okay." She sipped the hot brew as she tried to return to an inner calm. She must have convinced Monica because after watching her for several minutes, she went back to her desk.

Kayli couldn't go through this again. They had talked about the risk of drawing out the killer, but Shawn had been a near stranger at that point. Having an actual attack happen to a person she was coming to care for was a very different thing. They had to catch this guy before he harmed anyone else she cared for.

Chapter 13

Kayli found it harder and harder to go home to an empty house. Working late should have helped her forget her worry about Michael, and how she missed him, but it didn't. That smiling face, her arms around that wiggly body, bedtime stories, waking with his face two inches from hers. She sighed. Life was empty without her son.

Shawn. Another person to worry about. He'd come so close to being seriously hurt. Each time she thought of it, visions of Max being run down ran through her head. She didn't want to worry that next time Shawn might not notice the danger.

This wasn't working. Well, it had worked for a couple of hours. Maybe she could stretch her legs and get a cup of coffee. Or maybe she should just go home. She pushed her chair back then heard a sound, like something being set down just outside her door. Her heart pounded.

Then something clanged. The cleaning service. Maybe. The killer would be stealthier. She crept to the door. Her hand shook as she reached for the doorknob. Bucking up her courage, she twisted and cracked open the door and peeked out.

Her shoulders dropped and her breath left in a whoosh. She recognized Brad by the dark hair pulled back into a short ponytail. The janitor ran a cloth across the top of a filing cabinet.

Kayli stepped into the other room. "Hi, Brad."

He jumped and spun around, his hand to his impressive

chest. "Jeez, Kayli. I didn't realize you were here." He caught his breath. "I haven't seen you in ages." His eyes went from her head to toes and then back up to her face again. "Trying to beat a deadline?"

"No. I just didn't want to go home." She hadn't noticed before how attractive he was, probably because she'd been in her little cocoon with Michael the only one allowed in.

"Yours is the last office I have to clean and I'll be done in fifteen minutes. Do you want to go get a drink? Delay going home a little longer?" His blue gaze held steady on her face, a slight smile warmed her.

She'd never thought of Brad this way before. They'd shared an occasional conversation when she worked late. A couple of times, he surprised her by making her a cup of coffee at Monica's coffee station and brought it to her. If Shawn's face hadn't popped into her head, she might have said yes. And then, thinking of Shawn reminded her of the killer. Could Brad be that man? She found it hard to believe.

"No, but thanks," she told him. "I was just about to go home. I should be tired enough to sleep now." Giving way too much information. She was tired.

Brad shrugged. "Suit yourself. Have a nice night, Kayli." He turned back to his dusting.

~~~

Kayli touched a daisy in the basket sitting on the corner of her desk. Daisies and flowers in two shades of purple. Monica had been excited when Kayli carried them in that morning.

Shawn must have brought them when he came for the paper from her printer. She hadn't seen them when she got home the night before. The splash of color on the kitchen counter that morning had lifted her spirits. She smiled as read the card again.

I enjoyed last night. You're in my thoughts. Shawn

She ran her finger across Shawn's name.

Maybe Shawn was trying to tell her he wanted to date her for real. He'd brought the flowers to her house and not a public display of having them delivered to work.

Her cell phone rang. Kayli picked it up and smiled when she saw it was Shawn.

"Hi, Shawn. I love the flowers. Thank you."

"I thought you could use some cheering up."

"I'm looking at them right now and they're still cheering me up." She touched a flower again.

"I have news on the prints."

Kayli stiffened. "Good or bad?"

"Both. The paper from your home office has your hand print on it almost exactly like the one on the note. The one from your office has no prints."

"What does that mean?"

"The only way you could have put that paper in your printer was if you wore gloves, which means that the note from the killer was the bottom sheet of paper from your printer."

Kayli shivered and fell back against her chair back. "Which means he was in this office when no one else was. Why would he do that?"

"I assume to confuse the police. To make them wonder if *you* are responsible for what's happening."

It certainly confused her. "But why?" Kayli's voice was almost a wail.

"If the police think you're responsible, then they may not try as hard to find him. Al agrees with my idea of what happened."

Kayli snapped to attention. "Do you think this was just a way for him to tell me that he could get close to me? He'd know the police would analyze the letter."

"That could be it, too. So, back to who has access."

"I don't know. Quite often at lunch time, Monica and I are both out. We don't lock up then. So anyone who works here could come in. Anyone who's a guest of someone here could, too."

"You have to start locking up any time you're both gone. Make sure you tell Monica. What happens at night?" Shawn asked.

"We lock up and then only the cleaning people can get in. Oh." Could it be Brad? He'd have easy access to her printer at night. No one would know. He seemed interested in her.

"Kayli? 'Oh', what?" Shawn's voice had tensed.

"The cleaning guy, Brad, came in while I was here last night. I told him I was still here because I didn't want to go home and he asked if I wanted to go out for a drink."

"And did you?"

"Shawn! Of course not," Kayli said.

"Sorry, I had to ask."

"No. You didn't. You should have known." He was there on that first 'date' when pretending was so hard for her. He was there as she slowly opened up to him, as she spent more time with him and got more comfortable with him. He'd held her. They'd kissed. Did he think that she'd suddenly gone man crazy and any man would do? If that wasn't enough, any man she barely knew could be a killer.

There was a long pause. Kayli almost thought they'd been disconnected. "You're right," he said quietly. "I should have known. I'm sorry." He took a breath. Kayli could picture him running his hand through his hair. "What's his last name? I'll tell Al about him."

"I don't know. I'm sure the service can give Al the info."

"All right. And I *am* sorry, Kayli. I'll talk to you later."

Kayli set her phone down. She stared at the flowers on her desk. She should move them to the filing cabinet behind her. She touched a flower again.

He apologized. He sounded like he meant it.

She felt like a teenager again when she and Max had had a fight. Upset, sad, and worried that it was over. Shouldn't mature relationships be more—mature? She fell against the back of the chair, closed her eyes, and rubbed circles on her temples. They didn't have a relationship. And each passing day made her crave it more.

Chapter 14

A presence stopped in front of her desk, and Kayli glanced up, startled to see Shawn.

"Come to lunch with me." The words sounded commanding but the look on his face was a question, unsure of her response.

She stared at him. He leaned over the desk and gave her a quick kiss. "Please?" He started to pull away and Kayli reached around the back of his neck and pulled him back down, needing more. He scooted around her desk without breaking the kiss, looped his arm around her waist and pulled her out of the chair.

Shawn ended the kiss but pulled Kayli tighter. He laid his cheek against the top of her head. "I wasn't sure how you would react when I got here."

Maybe they *did* have a relationship.

Kayli slid a hand to his chest. She pushed a little to give her space so she could look at him. "After we hung up, I felt like a teenage girl who'd had a fight with her boyfriend." Shawn started to speak and Kayli put her fingertips over his mouth. She smiled. "It took a while to figure that one out. I was in a committed relationship since my teens, so I think I reverted to those dating days."

Kayli pushed up on her toes, removed her fingers from Shawn's lips and gave him a quick kiss. "This is all so new between us. I think we're both a little unsure of each other."

Shawn gave her a slow, sexy smile. "So does that all mean 'yes' for lunch?"

Kayli laughed. "Yes, it means 'yes' for lunch. Did you even listen to what I said?"

"Of course I did. You felt like a teenager. If I felt like a teenager, all I'd be thinking about is sex." He ran a hand through his hair. "Ah, sorry. I shouldn't have said that."

"It's all right. I already know about it."

His eyebrows climbed and her face warmed.

"Max and I had agreed not to have sex until after we graduated from high school. He made this elaborate surprise for the night of our graduation. After we'd done it, he said waiting was one of the hardest things he'd ever done. That sex was always on a boy's mind."

"I can't believe he told you that."

She shrugged. "So, it's not true?"

"Of course, it's true. I'm just surprised he told you." He cupped her cheek. "There's so much more I want with you."

She swallowed, not knowing what she should say.

He stepped away from her and took her hand. "So, let's go to lunch."

~~~

Shawn stopped in front of *Patrick's Irish Pub*. "I thought we'd eat here." Fear filled Kayli's eyes as they strayed to the diners eating at tables between the parking lot and the building. He quickly added, "But not outside."

She visibly relaxed. "This is fine."

They went inside and were seated in a booth. Irish music played quietly in the background. On the walls hung pictures, cottages in a green forest, waterfalls, and even a couple leprechauns.

After the waitress left with their order, Shawn tapped his fingers on the table, staring at them. "I have a plan, but I'm not sure you're ready for it." He glanced at her.

Kayli frowned. "What is it?"

"I want to stay at your house this weekend." Worry and excitement crossed her face. "In your guest room or Michael's room. I want this killer to think we're—intimate. I'm hoping it will escalate his actions, maybe upset him so much he'll make a mistake."

"He's already tried to kill you. I don't think I can take escalation."

"I'll be even more careful." He covered her hand with his. She stared at their hands, but didn't try to clasp his. In a cheery voice he said, "On Saturday, there's a street fair that I thought you would enjoy, and on Sunday, there's a special exhibit at the art museum."

"So, you don't want to just stay at my house the whole weekend?" Kayli's tension lessened.

Shawn squeezed her hand. "No, I think that would be too much temptation for me." He wanted to spend time with her, but didn't want to push her too far.

Kayli blushed and bit her lip.

"I didn't mean to make you uncomfortable," he said. "We can still do the day things and I'll just drop you at home after."

Kayli turned her hand over and wrapped her fingers around his. "No, we'll follow your plan." She stared him in the eye, her determination apparent. "You're right. It *will* provoke him, and that means I'll be a step closer to getting Michael home. I can do this."

"Okay. I'll come tonight at six-thirty. Do you like Chinese food?" He'd never had to tiptoe around a client before, but he'd never felt like this about a client. She was worth every effort to get to know her, to make her comfortable with him, and to let her know that he cared for her.

She'd done the hardest thing possible to protect her son,

by sending him away. Then she put herself in danger to bring this to an end. She was stronger than she knew.

Some would call it a flaw that Kayli still grieved her husband, but he understood. She loved with all her heart and soul. And maybe someday, he'd be on the receiving end of that love.

~~~

At precisely six-thirty Kayli's doorbell rang. She raced to her security panel and checked the screen that monitored her front door. Shawn stood on the doorstep, the strap of a duffle bag over his shoulder, and a paper bag in the other arm, staring up at the camera with a smile. Her breath caught. He looked good in dark jeans and light green t-shirt, even on this little screen. She rushed to the door and let him in.

"Hi, Shawn." Her heart fluttered, and her fingers tingled. Nerves. They'd had dinner at her house before and he'd been a perfect gentleman. She wasn't ready for more, but sometimes her thoughts had to be stopped from going to crazy places.

Shawn stepped up to her before she could step back and kissed her. Just a quick kiss, but it got her heart beating faster, especially after he said in a low voice, "Hi, pretty lady."

The kiss was probably for whoever might be watching, but the comment was just for her, and she tucked it away.

A deep breath calmed her racing heart. "I've got the table set in the dining room." And the lights dimmed and candles on the table. Maybe it was too much. She took a slow, deep breath to calm herself.

Shawn led the way, and set their heavenly smelling dinner on the table. Chinese. Michael's favorite, not pizza, like most kids his age. Kayli fluttered off toward the kitchen,

91

calling over her shoulder, "You can use the guest room, last room on the right. I'll get drinks."

Drinks poured, food packages opened, and nerves set in. Kayli fumbled, trying to pick up her fork. It was dinner, they'd done this twice before at her house, but this time was different. Shawn wouldn't be leaving. He'd sleep under the same roof, only steps away.

Concentrate on the food. Scoop out pork fried rice. Pick up a spring roll with her fingers. Spoon beef broccoli onto her plate, and a little sweet and sour chicken.

She glanced at Shawn and wished she hadn't. His plate already loaded, he seemed to enjoy a mouthful way too much. His expression kind of like one time when he'd kissed her. Great! She compared herself to food.

Eyes on her plate, she forked up some rice and ate it, then tasted the rest of the food. Shawn knew his Chinese restaurants. No wonder he'd had that satisfied expression.

She peeked at him and found him watching her. Her fork halfway to her mouth, she paused and lowered it back to the plate. She wouldn't be able to swallow.

Her imagination took over. He felt so good wrapped around her. She had to pull up his shirt and run her hands over his bare chest, slide her hands over his shoulders and push the shirt off. Let him open her shirt and feel his hands on her. If she had enough courage tonight, she'd slip into his bed.

But it wasn't lack of courage that stopped her. Guilt. Like she always felt when she thought of Shawn that way, but it wasn't overpowering like it had been before. Her heart was beginning to believe her head. Max would have wanted her to find someone else to love and share her life with. It was too soon to know if Shawn was that person.

Shawn brought her back to her surroundings. "I'm almost afraid to ask what you were thinking about."

"I don't think I want to say." Even though she'd dimmed the lights, he must see the blush.

"Whatever it is, it makes me want to do this." He reached behind her head and pulled her toward him. His lips touched hers and she surprised herself when the tip of her tongue tickled his lips. He deepened the kiss and soon they were both breathless.

Shawn leaned back, and it took minutes before his breathing slowed. He stared into her eyes and she wondered if he knew what she'd been thinking.

"Let's watch a movie," he said. "Not a chick flick. I don't think I need any more ideas."

Kayli blushed and nodded. They worked together to put away leftovers and dishes.

She led the way to the family room, picked up the remote control and sat down on the couch. She turned on the television and Netflix. Shawn sat snuggly beside her. They spent several minutes discussing the movie choices and settled on a mystery neither had seen before.

Once the movie started, Shawn put his arm behind Kayli and pulled her closer. She wiggled to get comfortable and he kissed the top of her head. She looked up at him, smiled then looked back to the movie. At one point, the movie heroine crept down a hallway in her friend's house when a man barreled out of a bedroom, pushing her aside so he could leave. It startled Kayli and she jumped. Shawn tightened his arm around her and held her hand.

This kind of reminded her of watching movies with Max. They'd sit like this with Max's arm around her. She felt safe with Shawn, like she had with Max. But Shawn smelled different, he felt different. Her feelings were different. It was a good different. She realized that she wasn't feeling guilty for having feelings for Shawn. She snuggled even closer to him, leaned her head on his shoulder, relaxed and turned her

93

attention back to the movie.

He kissed the top of her head again, and she gave his hand a squeeze.

The movie ended, and they discussed it for a while, until Kayli yawned. Shawn laughed and recommended that it was time for bed.

He must have noticed her worry. "Hey, remember, I'm sleeping in your guest room." He put his palm on the side of her face. "But, I can't resist a goodnight kiss."

She knew he meant short when he said goodnight kiss, but Kayli held on. He wrapped his arms around her and pulled her onto his lap. He deepened the kiss and both of their breaths quickened.

Finally, Shawn pulled back, and gazed into her eyes. "Are you trying to ruin my resolve?" He tipped his head up and pulled Kayli's head under his chin. He held her like that for a couple of minutes then slid her off his lap. She was both relieved and disappointed.

Shawn stood, stared down at her. "I'm going to bed now." He reached out, but pulled his hand back before touching her. "I'll see you in the morning."

He walk to the stairs and picked up his overnight bag from the bottom before heading up. He didn't look back. She watched until he disappeared. He went way too slow. She wanted to call him back. Maybe he'd adjusted his pace in hopes that she would.

This started because they needed to draw out a killer. She wouldn't have dreamed that a fake date would turn into real feelings. Maybe she was attracted to him because he'd broken through the barriers she'd had around her heart. She didn't know if that would have happened with any man given similar circumstances. She hadn't felt a need to go out in the last three years, and it would have continued without Shawn there to drag her into living again.

She sighed. Maybe Shawn was just very good at making clients comfortable. She didn't know if he'd had other romances during cases. And if it was as real as it felt, would Shawn be good for Michael? She sighed again and headed up to her bed.

Chapter 15

Kayli stepped out of her bedroom the next morning to the clatter of dishes and smell of sausage. It was nice to wake up with someone else in the house. It couldn't beat Michael being home, but Shawn was a close second. She entered the kitchen just as Shawn picked up two plates with eggs, sausage and toast. He smiled when he saw her and headed for the dining table, stopping to drop a kiss on her cheek before passing.

She liked those little kisses, signs of affection. If only every morning could start this way. "Thank you. I'll pour juice."

Over the meal, they talked about family and friends, but Kayli's most important family member wasn't with her. She could imagine Michael talking a mile a minute, telling Shawn all the things he wanted to do on the weekend. Her heart ached. She wanted her little chatterbox home.

Shawn covered her hand. "What's wrong?"

"Most of the time when I think about Michael, I just push the thoughts away. It's too hard thinking about him gone and wondering how he's coping. But, talking about family brings it all back. I want to talk to him again. I want this all over so he can come back home."

"It *will* be over soon. But, in the meantime, this weekend, I'll check over your computer and set up another Skype call."

"Thank you." Kayli blinked back tears.

In an overly bright voice he asked, "So, are you ready for

some street fair fun?"

~~~

They managed to find street parking several blocks from the fair. As soon as they opened the car doors, music surrounded them.

Kayli took Shawn's hand and squeezed it. "I've never been to a street fair."

The rhythm of steel drums led them to the crowd.

"I've come to this one for years. There's always something new." They passed the barriers blocking traffic. People crowded the street and sidewalks, several with well behaved leashed dogs. Doors of most of the stores were open, some had racks of clothing or other items on display. Vendors under canopies lined both sides of the street, selling locally made goods—jewelry, paintings, photographs, lotions, candles. They'd have to go back to some of them later, but now she wanted to see it all.

As they continued down the center of the street, the music grew louder. They stopped at the edge of a crowd to listen to a band playing Bruno Mars songs, finishing with a song she'd never heard before.

Kayli leaned into Shawn to be heard. "They're really good."

"They have to audition to perform. A couple of the bands have been discovered here, so it's gotten to be pretty steep competition." They listened to a couple more songs and moved on.

She stopped to watch groups of children play organized games. "Michael would love this. He loves competition, which is why sometimes he and Kim have disagreements. She just wants to have fun and Michael wants to win." She watched a determined boy win a sack race by about two hops.

The boy in second place had Michael's blond hair, and for a second, she thought it was him. She covered her mouth and fought back tears. Next year, she'd bring Michael.

Shawn squeezed her hand. He understood.

They walked a little farther and stopped at the edge of a crowd watching a juggler perform stunts. He circled on a unicycle as he tossed up a red ball and a yellow duck. He called out to an audience member who threw up another red ball, which he caught and put into his rotation.

Shawn leaned in. "There's a vendor passing with roasted nuts. I'll be right back."

Kayli nodded, her attention on the entertainment. She laughed and clapped. The juggler circled and reversed, changed his juggling pattern. The performance ended and the crowd dispersed. Shawn hadn't returned. She turned in circles, but couldn't find him. Worry set in. They hadn't planned on what to do if they got separated.

"Kayli. Imagine running into you here."

She knew that voice and whirled around. Better to face the man than have her back to him. "Hi, Dave."

He stood much too close, as always. He seemed to like invading her space. At the office, there were always coworkers nearby, unknowingly lending support, but the only person who knew her here was missing.

"Are you here alone?" Before she could answer, someone bumped Dave and his chest nudged Kayli's breast. He reached out and grabbed her arm as he righted himself. "Sorry." He didn't release her arm and Kayli tried to step back.

"So, are you here alone?"

She tugged her arm. "We got separated. Dave, let go." Panic started to well up. In the office, when Dave talked to her, she always felt a little uncomfortable, but his hand gripping her arm gave her horrible thoughts of being dragged between buildings. Her heart pounded and she unsuccessfully tugged her arm again.

"Yes, Dave. Let go," Shawn said with a hint of steel in his voice as he stopped beside Kayli and put his arm around her.

Dave released her like she'd burned him. "Sorry, man. I got pushed and I was catching my balance."

"Next time, don't." Shawn glared.

Dave lifted both hands as if Shawn had pointed a gun at him. He probably wanted to.

Again he said, "Sorry." Then turned and melted into the crowd.

Shawn turned Kayli to face him. "Are you okay?"

She nodded. "It's just—I don't know. I don't like the guy."

"How do you know him?"

"He's at the office. I try to avoid him, but if he spots me, he always stops to talk. He's a creep. Maybe he's the one. Monica's a close friend of Janice, the HR person. Janice told her that women from three companies have told the sales manager that they want to be assigned a new rep or they'd take their business elsewhere."

Shawn stared in the direction Dave had gone. "Yeah, he's definitely a creep. I'll find out from Al if Dave checked out and let him know about today."

Shawn squeezed her shoulder. "I'm sorry I left you. I was only a few steps away and I saw Dave talking to you, but with the crowd moving through, I couldn't get to you fast enough."

Shawn took Kayli's hand. "Let's leave it to Al and forget about him for now. Do you want some cashews?" He held a wax bag out to her.

She took a last look in the direction Dave had disappeared. It could be him.

Chapter 16

Sunday morning, Kayli dressed in black pants and a frilly mauve shirt. She came out of her bedroom to the heavenly aroma of bacon. She loved Shawn in her kitchen. "Waffles? You found my waffle iron?"

"I found it yesterday when I was looking for pans."

"And they're not sticking. How did you do that?"

He frowned. "Why would they stick?"

"I've never been successful with waffles. I follow the directions on the pancake box exactly and they always stick."

Shawn grinned. "That's your problem. *I* use my mother's secret waffle recipe. Perfect waffles every time. Unless you get distracted." He walked toward Kayli and kissed her. He ran his hands up and down her back. This was exactly what made mornings with Shawn perfect. Even better than breakfast.

"Mmm. Now back to the waffles." He turned back and popped two perfect waffles out of the iron and placed them on top of a stack in the oven beside the bacon. Then he poured more batter into the waffle iron.

By the time she finished setting the table, Shawn had grabbed the food from the oven and set it in the middle of the table.

Kayli loaded her plate and poured warm maple syrup over her waffles. Too many days of breakfast like this, and she wouldn't fit into her clothes.

Shawn cut his sausage. "Since the museum exhibit doesn't open until noon, I thought we could take a walk in the park or hike at the state park."

"I haven't been on a hike since—since Max and I went. I'd like that." She and Max had gone hiking frequently. They'd pop Michael into a baby backpack and Max carried him everywhere. She could picture Michael now, leading the hike, climbing hills and scrambling over rocks. He'd missed so much without his father. She wished Michael could be with them today.

Between the delicious breakfast and conversation with Shawn, she pushed past her sadness.

After stuffing herself, Kayli pulled two bottles of water out of the refrigerator for the hike.

Shawn closed the dishwasher. He was handy around the house, more than Max had been. Guilt grabbed her. Max had been wonderful. She didn't want to make comparisons where he came up short.

"I've got a backpack in my car and some trail mix," Shawn said. "If you want to change for the hike, we can come back here before going to the museum."

"All right. Give me a few minutes." She ran up the stairs, returned in shorts and a tank top, and found Shawn leaning against the front door, grinning at her.

They locked up and she followed him as they rounded the corner of the garage. He stopped suddenly and Kayli ran into his back.

"Damn! I expected a reaction, but not this."

"What's wrong?" Kayli stepped beside him, and gasped. "Shawn! Your car." She grabbed his arm. On the smashed windshield sat an envelope with her name laser-printed across it. Once they passed Kayli's Camry, she saw that the tires on this side were flat. Shawn checked the other side and his lips straightened to a line. He came back to Kayli and squatted down beside the front tire.

"It's been slashed." Shawn retrieved a pair of latex

gloves from his car, put them on and picked up the envelope. "Let's go back inside."

Before Kayli had the door open, Shawn was on the phone with Al. They went inside and locked up. "Al should be here in ten minutes."

At the security panel, Shawn pushed buttons until a fast reverse view of the driveway displayed. A man appeared on the screen. Shawn stopped it just after the guy disappeared. He reversed and slowed to normal speed. The time was three-ten.

A man dressed in dark clothes walked up the driveway. He ducked down and the car dipped on that corner. The man stood and did the same at the front tire. As he came around the front, he tipped his head up, revealing a ski mask. He knew about the cameras.

That was the man who'd taken Max's life, and he was still a mystery. What went through his head? Why would he do it?

He squatted and sliced the front tire with a large knife. He stood, walked to the back and did the same to the last tire. He slipped the knife into a sheath, then passed an object from his left to right hand, and walked to the front of the car. Kayli gripped Shawn's arm when she realized the man lifted a tire iron. He smashed it down on the windshield. She counted five times. Then he reached into a coat pocket and extracted an envelope, slipped it under the windshield wiper and walked away.

"Seeing this makes it worse. He had so much anger when he hit the windshield." She couldn't control the full body shake. "Do you think it was Dave?"

He put an arm around her, and reviewed the scene again.

"The build is similar. It's possible. Let's go sit." He led her to the couch, sat down beside her, and pulled her close. "That's just a car out there. It can be fixed. We're fine."

She let out a wobbly breath. "I know. It's just that he seemed so angry. And he was just somebody out there. Now he has a—not a face, but a body. And he's more real."

"And we're one step closer to finding him and getting Michael back. Now let's see what he has to say."

"Shawn, should we wait for Al?" Kayli bit her bottom lip.

"No, it's okay. I have the gloves on." He wiggled his fingers as the doorbell rang. "I guess we're doing it with Al after all."

Shawn opened the door and brought Al inside, indicating a chair across from her. Shawn resumed his seat beside her, except not quite as close as he had been.

"That was a pretty vicious attack on your car," Al said.

"Not as serious as when he tried to run me down."

"That's true. Did he leave that?" Al nodded to the envelope on the coffee table.

"Yes, we were just about to open it," Shawn said.

"Go ahead." Al leaned forward, elbows on knees, hands clasped.

Shawn pulled a small knife out of his pocket, slit the top of the envelope, and closed his knife. Then he pulled a sheet of paper out and dropped the envelope on the table. He opened the paper on the table.

Stay away from her or this may happen to her car while she's in it.

And then the fun really begins.

Her love belongs to me.

Kayli gasped, and gripped Shawn's leg then looked at Al. She hadn't feared for her own life before. If something happened to her, who would take care of Michael?

"Well, for the first time he reveals that he's not just trying to isolate Kayli," Al said. "Maybe he wanted to date you and you've rebuffed him. Now that you're dating someone else, he knows he has no chance, so he may be planning to kidnap you."

Kayli tightened her hand on Shawn's leg and shivered. Shawn put his arm around Kayli's shoulders and pulled her close to his side. Al glanced between them and frowned.

"Al, we have video footage of the guy damaging my car. He wore a mask so we weren't able to tell who he was."

"Shawn, can you have the security company send me the footage?"

"Of course. Maybe seeing it on a bigger screen will show something."

Al pulled a bag from his pocket and opened it and held it out to Shawn. "Do the honors?"

Shawn folded the letter, and dropped it and the envelope into the ziplock bag. Then he removed the gloves and stuffed them in his pocket.

Al slid the bag into his jacket pocket. "Shawn, come outside with me. I want a closer look at your car." He turned to Kayli. "I'd rather you stay in here." She nodded.

~~~

The men stopped beside the car and Al turned to Shawn. "Did you have to sleep with your client? She's vulnerable right now."

"I haven't. We planned this weekend to look like we're sleeping together. I slept in the guest room." He couldn't tell Al how much he *wanted* to have Kayli in his bed.

Al studied him and nodded. "You two seemed awfully close in there." He nodded toward the house.

Shawn forced a shrug. He didn't want Al to know how strong his feelings were for Kayli. "I care what happens to her."

Al stared at Shawn for a moment longer then turned to

104

the car. "I'm surprised there isn't body damage. At least it will be a relatively cheap repair." He leaned over the windshield. "There are fibers stuck in the glass. I wonder if he covered the—"

"Tire iron." Al hadn't seen the security video yet.

He nodded and squatted beside the closest tire and inspected the slice. He checked the back tire.

Shawn wondered what Al expected to see. All the tires had a gash in them. What more was there?

"Hey, Shawn, what do you think of this?"

Shawn squatted down beside Al. "What?"

Al pointed at a quarter under the edge of the car.

"It's a quarter." Shawn frowned. It could have gotten there in a hundred ways.

"Do you think Kayli dropped it?" Al asked.

"Probably not." Then Shawn realized what Al was getting at. "And I didn't drop it, so maybe the vandal did. Do you really think it would have prints on it?"

"We can only hope. Give me one of your gloves."

Shawn fished one out of his pocket and handed it over. Al pulled on the glove, picked up the quarter, and dropped it into a small evidence bag, then labeled it.

"I'm sending my tech out to check your car, then you can have it towed." As he returned to his car, he pulled out his phone.

Shawn went back inside.

"What did you two find?" Kayli asked.

"Al found a quarter."

"A quarter?"

"It was next to one of the tires so he thinks it may have been dropped by the vandal. Maybe it has prints."

"So, this guy might have finally messed up?" Kayli smiled.

"It might not be his quarter. Maybe his prints aren't in

105

the system. There could be no prints on the quarter. So, it's a slim chance."

"Shawn, don't ruin it for me yet. Your car is already ruined and our day is spoiled."

"My car's not so bad. There's no body damage, so I could have it back tomorrow afternoon. After the forensic guy looks at it, I'll have it towed to my garage." Shawn checked his watch. "It's too late to hike, but how about if we play cards, have lunch, and then go to the exhibit?"

"All right."

~~~

"Are you ready?" Shawn asked.

"Maybe we don't need to go. If Dave—"

"That's the thing. We don't know if it's Dave. He could just be an obnoxious moron. We'll play this out, just in case. Besides, you could use the distraction."

"Okay."

"Let me go change again."

He appraised her from head to toe. Perfect. "I think you look great just as you are."

She looked down at her clothes. "But not for the museum."

Within a few minutes, she returned in her original outfit. Still nice, but not as sexy.

"Maybe, we could..." Kayli caught her bottom lip between her teeth then hurried to the door beside the security panel and opened it.

Shawn followed and peeked into a garage. Two cars.

"Take that one," Kayli finished as she pointed to the car in the second bay with a cover over it.

"So, that's why you don't park in the garage. What's under the cover?"

"It's a 1970 Mustang. Max's grandfather gave it to his dad for graduation. Then his dad gave it to Max when he graduated."

"And it hasn't been driven for three years?" Shawn asked.

Kayli shook her head.

"I would love to use it today. But I don't think it should even be started until it has the oil changed and the gas replaced. Do you mind if I have a look under the cover?"

"Go ahead."

Excitement rushed through him. He loved Mustangs. It wasn't even his car, but he felt like he was unwrapping a present. He pulled back the cover on the nearest corner. Bright, shiny red. He flipped the cover off the other front corner and walked it back. "It's a convertible!" He'd bought the sensible cars, but he'd always wanted a convertible. Once the cover was totally off, he gave a long whistle. "This is impressive." He grinned at Kayli.

She smiled. "Max loved this car. I'd never sell it. I should probably sell this one." She patted the Subaru beside her. "It was just easier to close the door and forget."

His chest ached at her words. For three years, she lived only for her son. Now she'd cracked open her shell a little and shown him something about Max. Her lost love was still fresh for her. "Well, let me get this covered and we can get out of here." He fitted one corner of the cover on the rear bumper.

"I'll help." Kayli joined him.

Between them, they had the Mustang covered in a couple of minutes.

He wanted to wrap her in his arms, and tell her that he'd be there for her. Without trying, she'd worked her way into his heart, but hers was only beginning to heal.

107

Chapter 17

Three uneventful, lonely days later, Kayli was in her office, her thoughts on her son. It felt like forever since she'd held him. Shawn had set up Skype at home for her, and because he had work to do for Adam, she hadn't seen him since the weekend.

She and Michael had Skyped just before he went to bed the night before. It was bittersweet watching Jackie tuck him into bed. Kayli had read him a bedtime story, one of his many favorites. He fell asleep two pages before the end. She and Jackie had talked for a few minutes, and then she'd closed the connection. And cried. She drew in a deep breath and let it out slowly.

She had work to do, and had already used an hour feeling sorry for herself. She gulped down some coffee and pulled up a spreadsheet.

Her cell phone rang, a local number she didn't recognize. Her heart rate kicked up. Would her stalker call her? "Hello?"

"Hi, Kayli. It's Al Barnes. How are you?"

Relief, then alarm swept her. "Al? Is everything okay?" Usually she got information from Al through Shawn. Maybe Shawn had been hurt.

"Everything is fine, but can you come in this afternoon?"

"Why?"

"I'd like to discuss something with you without Shawn."

She gripped the edge of the desk. She had no idea what he had to say to her. Why would it be better without Shawn?

"How is four o'clock?"

"Perfect."

She dropped her phone on the desk. Shawn wouldn't be there. What did Al need to say to her that couldn't be said in front of Shawn? Maybe she should call Shawn anyway. She reached for her phone and pulled back. No. She'd do it on her own, but it worried her.

Throughout the day her thoughts kept straying to Al's call. He'd said everything was fine, but as the day wore on, the more she wondered if maybe it wasn't. She'd barely eaten lunch. At least, while she worked, she could mostly push those thoughts away.

Finally, it was time to leave. Kayli plodded into the police station, and was directed back to his office. She passed officers at desks. Almost all glanced up at her as she walked through. She hadn't noticed them the last time and wished Shawn was beside her.

Al glanced up when she stopped in his doorway. Three neatly stacked piles of papers lined the left edge of his desk. Another stack was scatter over his keyboard. He tapped them together and set them to his right. "Have a seat, Kayli." Al pointed at a chair in front of his desk.

Nerves took over. She couldn't read his expression.

He leaned forward and laced his fingers. "Kayli, I'm worried about this plan you and Shawn have been executing."

"I've been worried about Shawn since that car hit him, but he keeps assuring me that he can take care of himself." Al put his life on the line every day he walked out the door of the police station. Surely Shawn was as well trained.

"Normally he could—"

"What do you mean 'normally'?" Was there something that prevented Shawn from keeping himself safe? And shouldn't Al talk to Shawn about this?

A small smile flitted across Al's face. "It appears that the fake romance has become real."

Kayli blushed and looked down at her hands. "That was unexpected."

Al's chair squeaked. "Since it has, I'm worried that it may cloud Shawn's judgment."

Kayli whipped her head up and found him leaning forward. "What do you mean?"

Al's eyes narrowed. "Shawn may be so worried about you that he misses important clues and gets himself or you into serious trouble. There's a lot of danger around you, and everyone needs to be able to think clearly."

"What do you expect me to do, Al?"

His face held no expression, but his hand clenched into a fist. "Fire him. Break up with him, at least until this is over."

Kayli shook her head. "He wouldn't let me. I suggested we do a public breakup after the car hit him and he refused. Vehemently."

"But now there's been a direct threat to you, Kayli. He's got to see that he should back off."

"There's always been a threat to me."

Al opened his mouth to speak and Kayli raised her hand to stop him.

She stood. "I'll think about it, but I'm not making any promises."

Al leaned back. "Think long and hard about it, Kayli."

She nodded and left.

Kayli sat it her car, regaining her composure. Al had known Shawn longer than she had. Maybe he could see something she'd missed.

On her drive home, a pain started throbbing in her temples. With each repeat of Al's words, the pain intensified. Inside the house, she reset her security system and kicked off her shoes. She dropped flat on her back onto the couch, and dropped her arm over her eyes to block the light, hoping it might help her raging headache.

She knew Al was right—to a point. If she fired Shawn...She amended it. If Shawn let her fire him *and* they broke up, he *might* be safer. But she wouldn't be.

That guy was still out there. He wanted her and he wouldn't stop trying. She didn't have a choice. Shawn was the one who'd put himself in danger to protect her. She'd hired him to do exactly that. They were strangers when Shawn planned to trick the killer into reacting. If they were still only client and hired protection, she wouldn't even be thinking anything was wrong with this.

She sighed. Al thought that Shawn's judgment might be clouded. She didn't think so, but she wouldn't know if they'd missed clues. Despite the damage to Shawn's car, they really hadn't gotten any further in identifying this guy. They had to try something else. She let her mind sort through everything that had happened, a plan resolving. She jack-knifed up, then grabbed her head and moaned.

She just had to convince Shawn it was worth the risk to try it. After she took some ibuprofen.

Chapter 18

Kayli opened the door for Shawn. He pushed the door closed and put his arms around her. She tipped her head up and he kissed her.

"I'm glad you asked me to dinner. Do you realize that this is the first time that *you've* asked?"

Kayli nodded and bit her lip. "I have an ulterior motive that we'll discuss after dinner."

Shawn looked at her quizzically.

She shook her head. She wanted a pleasant meal with him before he blew up. "No, I'm not saying anything."

They sat at the dining table, and she told him about her call with Michael. He told her that he'd gotten his car back just a couple of hours earlier. A couple of times, he tried to ask what she wanted to talk to him about, but she cut him off. She was nervous enough that she hadn't really tasted the chicken primavera, but hoped Shawn had enjoyed it.

After the meal was over and cleared away, Kayli led him into the living room. "Okay, now I'm ready to talk." She hoped that sounded more confident than she felt.

Shawn sat on the couch and Kayli sat facing him with one leg drawn up.

His eyes narrowed, but he stayed quiet.

She sucked in a deep breath. Now or never. "Our plan has only worked to a point. We need to change it."

"This is working. He wrecked my car."

"But what else has it accomplished?" Kayli grabbed his hand. "We still don't know who he is."

"He'll slip up." He squeezed her hand. "We just need to give it more time."

"But will that happen before or after one of us is seriously hurt?" She stared down at there joined hands for a few seconds, gathering her courage, then up into his eyes. "I want us to do a pretend breakup."

"I've already said we're not doing that." He yanked his hand from hers.

"Why, Shawn?" She waited. In a louder voice, she repeated, "Why?"

"Because if I'm out of the picture, he'll be focused on you!" He turned his face from her, his mouth in a thin, tense line.

"I want to date—"

"We *are* dating."

"—other men." That had been harder to say than she'd expected, considering it was fake.

Shawn's head snapped around. "Kayli, what are you talking about?"

She hadn't expected the anger. He didn't understand it wasn't real.

She plowed on, needing to get the whole plan set out. "First I want to date Brad, the cleaning guy. I'll get a sense of what he's like and we'll see if I get any notes about him."

"You'd risk his safety to rule him out?" Shawn asked.

Kayli frowned. "I hadn't thought of it like that." She didn't want to put innocent men in danger. "You got a warning before the guy ran you down."

"You already know what he wants, so you might not get another warning."

He'd shot down her idea before she could explain it. "We need to do something to get this over with. It feels like it's going to go on and on for months or years and I'll never get Michael back." Tears threatened and she closed her eyes.

He pulled her onto his lap, wrapped his arms around her and rested his cheek on the side of her head. His closeness calmed her.

"Okay, we'll use your plan with my twist."

Kayli pulled away to looked at him.

"We'll do the pretend breakup. You'll mope for a few days." Shawn smiled when she frowned. "Hey, you lost a really great catch."

She punched his shoulder.

"Then you'll become promiscuous."

"*What*?"

"I showed you what you've been missing and now you can't get enough." He wiggled his eyebrows.

Kayli blushed and turned away. "Shawn, you're outrageous. I don't think I can do something like that."

"I listened to your plan. Now listen to mine," Shawn said. "I have friends and friends of friends who are police and ex military. They can take care of themselves. I want you to start picking them up at bars. You'll meet the first guy and spend the evening drinking. He'll follow you home and stay until about two and leave. The two of you could play cards or you can go to bed and he'll watch TV. We know what it's implying to whoever might be watching. A couple of nights later the two of you go out to dinner and repeat the rest of the evening. Then the next week, you'll do the same thing with another guy. Then on and on until this guy blows his top."

There was no way she could pretend to be a slut. She'd only been with one man. She wouldn't know how to even pretend to pick up a guy. "Shawn, this is crazy!" She barely recognized her raspy voice.

"Kayli, all you've got to do is talk to them."

"How will we know each other?" There had to be holes in this plan.

"You'll each get pictures and have each other's names."

She couldn't do this. No sense even asking questions, but she plowed on. "What if I'm there first and someone else sits down beside me?"

"Tell him you're waiting for your blind date. I'll tell everybody to go with that if someone is sitting with you."

"But that will spoil the plan that I'm trying to pick up a guy."

"Well, look him up and down and tell him you're not interested."

"Oh, great. Then I'll make somebody who's not the killer angry with me."

Shawn shook his head. "I'm sure it won't be the first time the guy gets rejected. Don't worry about it."

She leaned away from him. "Fine. Where will you be?"

"I'll be nearby, watching the customers."

"I can't believe I'm considering this." These would be guys that Shawn knew. They would know it wasn't a real date. That should be easier, but it wasn't.

"We wouldn't have to talk like we were going to end up back here, would we? I don't think I could do that."

"No. Just talk about whatever you're comfortable with."

Another thought struck Kayli. "I don't have any pick-up clothes."

Shawn laughed. "Not all guys like the hooker look. Let's go see what you've got."

"In my bedroom?"

Shawn lifted his eyebrows. "Is that where your clothes are?"

Kayli slapped his shoulder again and got off his lap. "Ok, let's look."

She led the way to her bedroom, gave a guilty glance to the other closet before she threw open her closet door and turned on the light. She'd never thought of her walk-in closet as being intimate before, or too small. She drew in a deep breath to steady herself and realized that was a mistake when all she smelled was Shawn.

Fortunately, he was scanning her clothes. "You're so organized." He ignored the left side of the closet, where her pants and suits hung, and stopped in front of skirts. "Dresses and skirts that are slim, so they'll ride up when you sit on a bar stool."

He seemed to be getting into this, and didn't mind that she'd be showing her legs to strangers. Maybe she minded.

He pulled out three skirts that met his requirements and handed them to Kayli. He turned back to the clothes. "Sleeveless shirts to show off your sexy shoulders. Ah, a halter top."

Shawn turned with a filmy blue-green top. That expression. He was imagining her wearing it, which made her imagine wearing it for him. It was getting way to hot in her closet.

"Do you have one of those push-up bras?" he asked.

"Shawn!" Kayli blushed.

He laughed and handed her the blouse, then turned back to the shirts. "Oh, I like this shade of purple." He ran a finger along the neckline in front. "Low, but not too low."

She grew warm where his fingers might have been if she'd been wearing that shirt when he did that. She let out a breath. Shawn studied her. "Are you okay, Kayli?"

"I'm fine," she answered quickly. Shawn handed her the shirt and turned back.

"And this gold one. I bet it's not really as low as it looks." He handed it to her. "Now dresses." He pulled out a royal blue backless dress. "I love this. Too sexy for them. We'll save it for me." He hung it back up as Kayli tried to smother a chuckle. He pulled out another dress. "Oh, you wore this on our first date. It should do for another dinner date." He handed it to her.

It surprised her how much she was pleased that he remembered it.

Kayli pushed aside some clothes on the rod nearest the door and hung up the clothes that filled her arms. When she turned back, Shawn contemplated a dark green dress. Tags hung beside the sleeve. "Now this—"

"No! Put it back!"

Shawn quickly hung it up and held her loosely in his arms. "Kayli, what's wrong?"

She closed her eyes and gasped in quick breaths. "Max bought it for me. I was going to wear it on our anniversary."

Shawn stared at her. Something she didn't understand flitted across his face.

He pulled her closer. "Kayli, I'm glad that you had such a wonderful relationship with your husband. I wish this insane guy hadn't taken him from you."

Kayli tightened her arms around him. He wasn't threatened by a ghost.

He drew in a breath. "Let's go back downstairs."

Back in the living room, Shawn said, "I should go. Lunch tomorrow for our argument?"

Kayli nodded. "All right. Call me and I'll come down. Um, Shawn." She looked down and then back up at him. "Since we can't kiss and makeup afterward, can we kiss now?" She had no idea when they'd get to again.

Shawn put a finger under her chin and tipped her head up. "I think that's a great idea." He slowly moved closer. He was taking too long. Kayli threw her arms around his neck and kissed him. He ran his hands up her back, and she melted into him. Finally, he pulled back, his breaths sawing in and out. "It's good I've got all night to prepare for the argument because I sure couldn't yell at you now."

Kayli smiled. "I'll have to remember that."

He stood at the door with his hand on the knob. "I wish

117

we didn't have to do this."

She touched his neck and kissed his cheek. And then he was gone.

Somehow, it already felt like they'd broken up.

~~~

Kayli paced her office. Nerves kept her in motion. She'd been all right most of the morning, but the closer lunch time and the argument came, the harder it was to concentrate. Her cell phone rang, and even though she was expecting it, she jumped.

She snatched it off her desk. "Shawn."

"Hi, Kayli. I'm just outside your building. Are you ready for this?"

She sighed. "As I'll ever be."

"When you see me, I want you to give me a kiss on the cheek and try to take my hand. I won't let you. And we'll go from there."

"Okay. I'm coming down." She tucked her phone in her purse and slung the strap over her shoulder.

Shawn jumped up from the bench near the door when she came through the doors. She kissed his cheek and when she reached for his hand, he slipped it into his pocket. She frowned at him and started walking toward the food cart.

He took her arm and turned her to face him when they were almost there. "I need to tell you something."

She tipped her head. "What?" This didn't sound like the start of an argument, but he couldn't have changed his mind in the few minutes since the phone call.

"I don't want to see you anymore."

"What? Why?" She made it a bit louder than she might normally have, and reached out to take his arm, but he shrugged it back.

People walking by stopped to watch and she did her best to ignore them.

"You were fun and games, but you're not worth it any more." His voice, a little louder than hers. "I got hit by a car and my vehicle was destroyed because of you."

She grabbed his arm, but when he pulled this time, she held on tight. "I thought we had something special." She wasn't doing this very well. She should be yelling at him, showing anger, but she only felt pain.

"Not special enough to risk my life."

"Well then, you're not worth it either," Kayli yelled. She snatched a bottle of ketchup from the cart and squeezed it, spraying his chest with red. "And find another food cart. I don't want to see your face any more."

Shawn stood, stunned for a second as she glanced between the bottle in her hand and his shirt. She was just as surprised as he was.

He pulled out his phone and started pushing buttons. His voice now under control. "I'm deleting your number. I don't want to see you either." He stalked off down the street.

Kayli slammed the ketchup bottle on the cart and headed back to her office. A round of applause startled her, but she couldn't turn to look.

Good. Monica had left for lunch already. She closed her door and leaned back against it, and giggled. The look on Shawn's face when she squirted ketchup on him was priceless. Suddenly, she couldn't keep her legs under her, and dropped into the chair in front of her desk.

Her cell phone rang. Shawn. No surprise there.

She hit *talk*. "Hi, Shawn."

"Are you okay? For a bit there, it looked like it was all too real for you."

She let out a breath. It was her caring Shawn. "It was. You're way too good at it. I'm sorry I squirted ketchup on you. It just happened." She giggled. "But it was kind of fun."

He chuckled. "Yeah. I was totally taken by surprise. In the future, if we ever have an argument, just say, 'ketchup' and it'll be over."

"Okay. Another thing I should remember." She loved that he said 'in the future'.

"I'll call you in a couple of days, after I've set up your first pick-up. I still can't believe I let you talk me into this."

"Shawn, this is going to work." She dropped her phone on the desk. It was sinking in. They'd done the first step, and in a few days, she'd be pretending to pick up a stranger and hoping a killer was watching. She shivered.

Chapter 19

Kayli breezed through Monica's office on Friday and hung her bag of date clothes in the closet in her office. She didn't want her secretary to see it and question her.

A few minutes later, Monica stood in the doorway. "Next Thursday is the first *Concert in the Park*. The band is called *New Earth*. Do you want to go?"

She didn't know how to answer. It could be fun, and she was supposed to have broken up with Shawn, so she had the time. She needed to break out of another Max memory. If she hadn't spent so much time with Shawn, she would have outright said no.

"I checked out their website," Monica said. "They're good. And it will…take your mind off other things."

She needed this, and it was nice of Monica to think of her. "Okay. Dinner, too. Right?"

Monica beamed. "Yes. And it's going to be so much fun. I'll bring a blanket." She went back to her desk.

~~~

Kayli had waited until Monica left work that evening before changing for her 'date'. She'd had to tell her about the breakup with Shawn that same afternoon, so that it could make its way through the grapevine, but there was no way Monica would believe Kayli would go trolling for a stranger.

She nervously ran her hands down the slim navy blue skirt. She hadn't worn it since before she had Michael

121

because it was now a little tighter in the hips than she liked. She turned and inspected her backside in the mirror. Guys wouldn't mind at all. The flowered blouse hugged her breasts and dipped just enough to display her braided gold chain.

Shawn had called yesterday to tell her he'd set it up. She almost wished they hadn't agreed to do it. Everybody in the bar would probably be able to see how nervous she was. The only thing that had gotten her this far was reminding herself that it brought her one step closer to getting Michael home.

She left the bathroom and came face to face with Brad. He stopped with his cart in a doorway.

"Hi, Kayli. I should thank you."

She gave him a puzzled look. "Thank me?"

"Yeah. A few weeks ago when I asked you out for a drink, I decided to go out anyway, even though my original plan was to go home. I met someone." His face lit up.

Kayli smiled. "And if you'd gone with me, you wouldn't even have noticed her. That's great, Brad. I hope it works out." She was glad they could strike Brad off the list. He'd always been sweet, and it looked like he truly cared for this girl he'd met.

He glanced at the clothes draped over her arm. "It looks like you're going out."

"Um, yeah. I sort of have a blind date."

"Well, I hope it works out, too."

"Thanks. Me, too." Just not the way he thinks. "See you later, Brad." She returned to her office, and picked up her purse and cell phone. She scrolled to the picture of Jeff that Shawn had texted her and her nervousness returned. He was way too attractive. Dark curls and dark eyes, a half smile, and really nice lips. But whatever drew her to Shawn, Jeff didn't have. She took a deep breath and headed out the door.

The parking lot in front of *Mickey's Tavern* had her choice of spaces, so she chose one only steps from the door.

A glance at her watch showed she was a few minutes early. She stared at the building. She'd never actually been in a bar before. Sure, she'd been in a restaurant bar while waiting for a table, but this was a real bar and she'd be alone at first. She hoped every eye didn't turn to her when she walked in. She'd probably stumble and fall flat on her face.

She reviewed what Shawn had told her. Step inside, stop and look around. Then slowly proceed to the bar, swing her hips a little, but not too much. Keep looking around, but don't make it too obvious. If possible, take a seat at the bar with an empty seat on each side of her. Let Jeff be the one to approach her.

Kayli inhaled and got out of the car. Remember, this was for Michael. She practiced her walk to the door and by the time she opened it, she felt more comfortable with the way she moved. She took two steps and stopped.

It was a sports bar. Large TVs on all the walls displayed different games in progress. She spotted the bar and started walking toward it.

She scanned the customers. A couple of men had noticed her already, and she shifted her eyes away so they couldn't make eye contact. Most men were there with other people. A couple more, who were alone, glanced at her and away. Another, she accidentally made eye contact with, and he seemed to appraise her. She caught sight of Shawn. He smiled just a little and then slid into the shadows of the booth. She almost stopped, but pushed past.

Some of her nervousness eased knowing he was near. Three empty barstools beckoned from the side of the room closest to Shawn. Good. She had to lift a little to get her butt on the seat and put her foot on the rail to finish sliding back. Hopefully that was graceful enough. She itched to wiggle her skirt down, but refrained.

Kayli turned to face the bar, but had no idea what to

order. An occasional glass of wine with a meal was the extent of her alcohol knowledge. Maybe they didn't even serve it.

The bartender stepped in front of her. "What can I get for you, pretty lady?"

"Um. I'm not sure. I don't like beer. Do you have a recommendation of something that's not too strong?" He gave her some suggestions and she made her choice. "And could I have an appetizer? Chicken strips?"

After he walked away, Kayli turned around to scan the room. She could just make out Shawn in his booth. Out of the corner of her eye someone stood from a barstool down several from her. She turned and saw that it was Jeff with a drink in his hand. She gave him what she hoped was a sexy smile. He smiled back and walked toward her.

"Mind if I take this seat?" he asked.

"It's free."

"I'm Jeff. What's your name?" He held out his hand.

It surprised her that he wanted to shake hands, like this was a business meeting. She extended hers as she said, "Kayli."

He gently held her hand and then caressed the top of it with his other hand and slid it up her arm. No, this was not a handshake. She pulled her hand and he released it. He sat beside her and set his drink on the bar. He turned slightly toward her and leaned close so that she could hear his lowered voice.

"I don't think Shawn appreciates my pickup routine." He chuckled.

"How do you know?"

"You should have seen the look on his face when I ran my hand up your arm." He chuckled again. "You're more than just a client, aren't you?"

She nodded. "It *has* turned into more." She turned back to the bar, finding her drink sitting on a napkin, and took a tentative sip, pleased with her choice.

"Well, he's going to have a *really* hard time later."

If Shawn was going to have a hard time, then she would, too. "Why?"

"We can't just talk for a while and leave together. To make it look like a real pickup, we'll have to touch each other. Make it look like we *have* to leave so we can do even more."

Kayli nodded and looked away from him. "This is going to be harder than my first fake date with Shawn." She turned back to him. "It was the first time I went out with a guy since my husband died three years ago."

"I'm sorry, Kayli. Shawn didn't tell me that." He put his hand over hers.

She relaxed a little at his understanding. "Okay, so we should look like we're enjoying each other." She smiled at him.

Jeff ran a finger down her cheek. "You have a beautiful smile. Sometimes I try to impress the ladies by telling them about my company."

Kayli jumped when the bartender set her chicken fingers beside her. She chuckled, pulled the plate closer to them and nibbled on one. She turned her stool so that her knee touched Jeff's leg. "So, tell me about your company." Maybe he liked to impress with his money.

It broke the ice and they jumped from topic to topic. Twice Jeff ordered more drinks. He leaned toward her. "I'm going to put my hand on your skirt and slide it down to bare skin. After a couple of seconds, I want you to put your hand on my thigh and slide it up as far as you're comfortable. Okay?"

Kayli nodded. She was glad of the warning. Although they'd touched each other's arms while they were talking and her knee was against Jeff's leg, this was totally different.

Most observers might think that her quickened breathing was a sexual response, but Kayli was trying hard to control a panic attack. "Are you okay?" Jeff whispered.

"Just give me minute." Her breathing slowed and she touched Jeff's leg. She moved her hand up a couple of inches.

He put a curled finger under her chin and lifted. "Let's go now. Shawn said a key thing is to have my car in your driveway for a while, so I'll follow you home."

She wondered if Shawn had told Jeff what happened to his car when it was in her driveway too long.

Kayli nodded and they stood. Jeff took her hand. She glanced at Shawn as they walked passed. He looked like he could kill Jeff. This was all *his* idea. She didn't feel bad for him, but was sort of glad that he was jealous.

In the parking lot, Kayli pointed out her Camry, and he walked her to it. She beeped to unlocked it and he opened her door. "Kayli, I'm going to touch your face now." He placed his hand on her cheek, and stepped close. If he'd done this the moment they'd met, she would have panicked, but he'd been thoughtful. It was almost like a brother-in-law hug. "If someone's watching, they'll think we're kissing," he whispered. He stepped back. "I'll be right behind you."

Kayli calmed as she drove home. The worst was over and it hadn't been bad. Jeff had been careful with her, treated her as if she was fragile.

She pulled into her driveway and Jeff parked beside her. He rushed to her car door, and opened it. He helped her out, and pulled her towards him, leaving about a six inch gap. Then ran his hand up her hand to the back of her head.

"There's a Jeep wrangler with an occupant about three doors down. Do you think it's a neighbor?"

She didn't turn to look. "I haven't seen it in the neighborhood before."

"Looks like our tryst at the bar wasn't needed," he whispered inches from her face.

It had worked already. Or maybe he would have been parked on her street even if she hadn't gone out. A chill enveloped her, thinking of being all alone with him out there. She hoped it wouldn't cause a problem for Jeff. Or maybe a neighbor had company.

He moved closer. "I want him to get the right impression."

Kayli put her hand on Jeff's shoulder then slid it around the back of his neck.

"Now, take my hand and lead me inside."

Once they were in the house, Kayli kicked off her shoes, sat on one end the couch and flopped back, staring at the ceiling. The couch gave as Jeff sat at the other end.

She sighed. "You must think I'm a real novice at dating." She glanced over at him.

"A pickup is not dating. A date with your husband isn't dating either."

Kayli stifled a yawn.

"Why don't you go on up to bed? Lock your door, if you'd feel more comfortable. I'm sneaking out the back to have a look at that Jeep. I'll talk to the guy, and then come back and watch TV for a while."

Kayli nodded. As she leaned forward to stand, the phone in her purse rang. "I wonder who that is?" she asked sarcastically as she reached down and rummaged in a pocket for her phone. "Oh, look. It's Shawn."

She smiled as she accepted the call. "Hi, Shawn. Did you survive the evening?"

"What were you doing?" He sounded almost angry.

"Shawn, you asked me to pick up a guy and I got one."

Jeff laughed.

Kayli interrupted his tirade. "It's been an exhausting

evening, so I'm going up to bed now. Alone. Do you want to talk to Jeff?" She handed the phone to him.

"Hold on, Kayli. Can you do dinner Tuesday?" She nodded. "I'll pick you up here at six-thirty." She nodded again and fled up the upstairs.

Before she closed her door, she caught a few words. "Shawn, I'm going out to check on a suspicious car up the block. Keep this short."

She'd done it and it had worked. They were one step closer to finding this killer and bringing Michael home.

Chapter 20

On Sunday morning, Kayli was working on a crossword puzzle, trying to keep her mind off Michael. Even the puzzle conspired against her with clues about children's games.

Her phone rang. Shawn. She almost didn't want to answer. He'd been angry the last time they spoke. She sighed and pushed talk.

"Hi, Shawn."

"Kayli."

She didn't get a sense of his mood from one word. "Yes, Shawn?"

"I'm so sorry I was an idiot the other night. My eyes contradicted what I knew in my head and I...I'm sorry."

"Shawn, you can't even know how hard that was for me. I had to walk into a bar. Alone."

"I was there already." Now he sounded defensive.

She sighed. "But not *with* me. Guys probably wondered who I'd be going home with. I don't *want* people thinking like that about me."

"But that's the impression we wanted you to make. And you did it beautifully." Now he sounded too excited.

"And if Jeff hadn't joined me so quickly, I probably would have turned around and walked back out. So, stop being angry with him!"

"I'm not. It was just a knee-jerk reaction. He was too convincing."

"He was sweet and patient, explaining what we were going to do. He warned me before he touched me."

Goosebumps rose as she remembered the occupied car on her street. "Oh, and it turned out that we didn't even have to do all that. The guy was parked up the street when we got home."

"Jeff told me, but the car drove off before he had a chance to confront him. At this point, we don't know if it's the stalker. A guy came in a short time after you got to the bar, and almost never took his eyes off you. He left a little before you did. I got the feeling he was angry with you."

A shiver went down Kayli's spine. She thought that feeling of being watched was only because Shawn was watching. Maybe they'd found the killer their first time out.

"If he left before me, he could have gotten to my house first." Somehow it seemed worse to be observed in both locations.

"It's possible."

"Does this change anything?" Maybe they were two steps closer, and she wouldn't have to do it again.

"No. You'll still go out with Jeff on Tuesday and meet a new guy on Friday. We really need to push him."

"Oh, I haven't had a chance to tell you. I ran into Brad, the cleaning guy at the office. He was so excited about his new girlfriend. I think we can cross him off the list."

"Don't be so quick. Maybe he's just trying to make you jealous. What does he look like?"

"He has dark hair that he pulls back into a ponytail, and—"

"If this is the guy, it's not him. He has a very neat, blond hairstyle. I'd send a picture, but none of them turned out."

They talked about other things and Kayli lost track of time. Her stomach growled and she glanced at the clock. "Shawn! We've been talking for nearly two hours."

"Oh, wow. I'm late. I'm supposed to be at Adam's house already to watch the game. I'll talk to you in a couple of days."

She set the phone down, and smiled at all they'd talked about. She'd been in a balloon and had finally popped it. Her life was more than just her and Michael. Max had been an important part of her life and she'd been only half awake for far too long. Shawn had so carefully broken through the walls and she couldn't imagine going back to the way she'd been.

Happiness. That's what she'd been missing.

Even when she was doing something fun with Michael, there was always a part of her heart that she'd closed off, an underlying sadness.

Kayli felt a deeper love for Michael. She wiped a tear from her cheek. She hadn't realized that she wasn't giving him as much love as she could. That she'd been holding back, trying to protect herself. When they caught this killer and Michael was home again, life would be so much fuller than it had been.

It was time. She stood and ran her hands down the front of her pants then marched into the garage and flipped on the light. A scan of the back wall yielded a stack of flattened boxes behind a group of paint cans. She tugged a few out then grabbed a roll of packing tape from a shelf.

In her bedroom, she assembled and taped two boxes, then tentatively stepped into Max's closet, on the other side of the bathroom, and dropped them on the floor. Kayli closed her eyes striving for calm. It had been almost three years since she'd opened this door. She was ready. Probably.

All she could manage were shallow breaths. Max's scent enveloped her in this small space, surrounded by his clothes. She'd almost forgotten what he smelled like. His love, his voice in her head, were like a hug. Her hand hovered over the light switch. Reality would return when she flipped it on. Only the light from the bedroom window lit the space. She'd been in this closet one last time after Max died to put away clean clothes.

With tears on her cheeks, she hit the switch and glanced at the clothes. Max's clothes. Suits, shirts, sweaters, ties, belts. Amongst his things, she felt closer to him than she had in a very long time, but still oh, so far.

She pulled a deep breath into pain filled lungs. She could do this. Sweaters filled the first box and half the second. Then from a drawer she pulled out a stack of t-shirts and added them to the second box. A second stack of shirts topped off the box. She dragged them to the bedroom, taped and labeled them, and assembled the next two boxes.

Back in the closet, she grabbed a bunch of shirts on hangers from the bar. She accordioned them into a box, followed by two more bunches of the shirts. She pulled all the ties off the rack, folded them together and shoved them down the side of the shirt box. In the next box she piled up jeans, sweat pants and a couple of sweat shirts. Kayli hauled the boxes out and prepared two more.

She pulled out a suit and folded it into a box. Then another and another, filling the first box. Two more suits went into the second box and then there was just a suit jacket. She pulled it down and, flattened it against herself, feeling a lump in the pocket.

Kayli reached in and pulled out a small gift wrapped box and an envelope. She held the jacket out at arm's length and stared at it, picturing it tossed into the backseat of the car. She dropped it on the floor and stared at the envelope.

Happy Birthday was written in Max's sprawled handwriting, reminding her of the little notes he'd leave in odd places—taped to the bathroom mirror, stuffed in her purse, on her car seat.

Her legs gave out, and she dropped to the floor. Max had left his jacket in the car when they had her birthday lunch. He said that when they were done eating he had to get something from it. Tears dropped onto her hands and the envelope and box she held so tightly. With shaking hands, she tore open the envelope and through her tears read Max's last message.

Happy Birthday, Kayli. I cherish every moment I spend with you. Let's celebrate each day together as if there is no tomorrow. Love, Max

Kayli jumped up and ran to the bed. She threw herself on it and sobs racked her body. She curled into a ball on her side. Her hands tucked close to her heart, still holding the card and box. Just when she thought she'd accepted Max's death, this gift crushed her. It brought back the feelings of love they'd shared. She'd buried them. It was the only way she'd been able to go on living. Max was gone. She'd never see him again or feel his love. Michael would never know the love of his father.

She fell into an exhausted sleep.

~~~

Kayli woke slowly in the dim room. The sun was setting. She pushed herself up, blinking her gritty eyes and rubbed at the dry tears on her cheeks. She slid off the bed and went into the bathroom, stared at the ravaged face. Her eyes were red and swollen. Her hair was a disaster. She put a hand to her heart. Even her chest hurt.

She splashed cold water on her face then patted it dry. She worked a brush through her tangled hair. A deep breath helped prepare her for what she still needed to do.

Back in her bedroom, she stared at the card and box on the bed. She forced herself to walk to the bed and sat on the edge. With trembling hands, she picked up the box. Maybe she wasn't ready to see what was inside.

For three years, Max's last gift lay hidden in a pocket. For many minutes, she held it. Max bought this gift for her.

She needed to see it.

Slowly, she unwrapped it, almost afraid something terrifying would burst from it. The name of a jeweler graced the box. Her fingers slipped on her first attempt to open it.

Inside, she found a necklace, a gold chain with a pendant. A circle of diamonds enclosed a much smaller offset gold circle attached to one side.

Max had taped a small paper into the top of the lid. *This diamond circle represents our love surrounding the gold circle of Michael.*

Tears stung her eyes as she touched the spot where the small and large circles met. She removed the necklace from the box and put it around her neck. The cold metal warmed as if Max had reached out to her. She kissed the diamond circle then pressed it against her chest. He'd designed an amazing love filled gift.

And his son would grow up, never having felt how much his father loved him.

Kayli lifted her head toward the ceiling. "Max, a part of my heart will always love you, but I'm ready to move on." She blinked back more tears and stood. The heavy weight she'd carried for so long lifted.

Returning to the closet, she packed the remaining clothes. Just before sealing the box, she retrieved from her closet the last dress Max had given her, and carefully laid it on the top then taped the box closed.

One by one, she carried the boxes downstairs and loaded them into her car. She closed the door and let out her breath. She would drop them off at Goodwill on her way to work. Then she'd call her mechanic about the cars, too.

~~~

Kayli paced as she waited for Jeff to arrive for their

Tuesday date, and thought back on the Skype call she'd had with Michael. The first one since she'd let go of Max. He'd given her an impish grin, and she'd noticed for the first time that it was Max's smile. It hadn't hurt. It had felt good to know that she still had a living, breathing part of Max. Maybe she hadn't wanted to see the likeness, or maybe her son looked less like a little boy. He needed to be home.

The doorbell rang, and Kayli gave one last inspection of her dress. Longer than the one she'd worn to the bar, the black and gold dress hugged her breasts and waist, and flared at her hips. Hopefully, it was appropriate for this type of date. Her nerves weren't nearly as bad tonight, since she wouldn't have to parade in front of a crowd. It was just another fake date with a likeable companion.

Kayli pulled the door open and watched a slow smile spread on Jeff's face. "I'm going to enjoy escorting you tonight. It's probably a good thing it's not real."

She blushed.

He held his hand out and she placed hers in his warm one. "Well, let's get going. Do you like Mexican?"

"I love it."

Jeff made her at ease with small talk, but he stayed alert, his eyes darting between the windshield and mirrors. He didn't say anything, and didn't give away if they were being followed. He made one of several turns, and his eyes flitted to the rearview mirror. "Gotcha!"

She started to turn, wanting to see what he'd seen.

"Don't look behind you," he said.

"He's back there?"

"Yeah. I chose this restaurant because it's out of the way. It's not likely someone would stay behind us for all those turns unless they were following us."

"What are you going to do?"

"There's not much we *can* do yet. Following isn't a

crime. And he could just say this is where he was coming, too." He pulled out his phone and dialed. "Hey, Shawn, we're almost there. The car behind us is suspicious. Take a look when we pull in."

As they turned into the parking lot, she looked around, and didn't see Shawn. The car behind them passed by and turned at the next corner.

"What'd you get, Shawn?"

Kayli hadn't realized that they were still on the phone.

"Maybe he'll come back."

Jeff frowned. "All right, see you later."

He put his phone away and got out of the car, joining her at her door.

"What did he say?" she asked.

He turned back. "He couldn't get the plate number. The guy didn't have his lights on and it's just dark enough to not be able to see it clearly."

"Since he drove by, he knows where we are. Can't we just leave?"

He grinned. "We've got to eat anyway, and they have great food here."

"Can Shawn join us?" Kayli would enjoy being able to talk to Shawn in person, even with someone else present.

"Sorry. The guy could circle the block and come back after we're inside. We have to make it look good. Shawn's going to stay outside to see if he can get the plate if he does come back."

"I guess that makes sense." She couldn't hide her disappointment.

"Hey, we've already spent an evening together. I don't still scare you, do I?"

Kayli defended herself. "I wasn't scared, just nervous."

He pulled the door open and gestured inside. "Let's go in or we'll be late for our reservation."

Kayli was amazed that they got all the way to their booth without touching. Then she remembered that they didn't have to put on a show yet. She sat down and slid to the middle of the bench, then Jeff sat opposite her. The hostess set the menus down in front of them and glared at him. "Amy will be your server."

"Great!" Jeff said with a tight smile.

"That didn't sound great. What's wrong?" Kayli asked.

He ran his fingers through his hair, messing it a little. "Amy doesn't normally work Tuesday nights."

She glanced around the room, trying to pick out the staff. "You know her?"

"Probably not anymore." Resignation in his voice.

"Oh." This must have been the best located restaurant for Jeff to risk his relationship.

Just then, a short, curvy woman with shiny brown hair curled around her ears stopped at the table, pen poised over a small pad.

"Uh, hi, Amy." Jeff said.

Her eyes bore into him, then flicked to Kayli and back to him. "She better be your sister." She stalked away before he could respond.

Kayli slid out of her seat and pointed at Jeff. "Stay there." She followed Amy.

"Hold on, Amy. I need to explain." She didn't want to be responsible for another couple breaking up

Amy turned with an angry glare.

Kayli pointed to a hallway. "In the lady's room. Lead the way."

Amy hesitated and finally nodded. Kayli followed her. She didn't want anyone else to overhear the explanation just in case that guy had come back.

Once they were inside, Kayli made note of the two stalls with the doors ajar. At least they were alone. "Jeff's working."

Amy crossed her arms. "And you're his secretary?"

"No. His friend, Shawn Gordon, is a PI. I hired him and we needed to set something up to look like I was a . . . dating several men." Amy didn't need to know the whole story.

"I know Shawn." She seemed a little calmer.

"So, I'm not dating Jeff. We're just making it look like I am. You can't tell anyone it's not real. We can't have it get back to the guy who's stalking me. Can you keep it a secret? Please."

"You're not dating Jeff?" Amy smiled then frowned. "He didn't tell me about this. He just told me he had something to do tonight, which is why I took this shift when one of the girls called in sick."

"I'm actually interested in Shawn."

"He's a nice guy. If I hadn't met Jeff first, maybe…"

No, maybe. He was hers. "I better get back to the table."

Kayli sat down across from Jeff. "Amy understands. She's okay with it."

He relaxed back against the seat. "Thanks, Kayli. I don't think she would have believed me."

"Why didn't you tell her?"

"The first time, Shawn sprung it on me and there was no time to tell Amy. And now, I'm seeing Amy tomorrow night, so I figured I'd tell her all this then. Which should have been before the girls had a chance to tell her they saw me."

"Before is always better."

"Got it." He scanned the restaurant. "Let's see if we can get Amy to take our order." He waved at her.

After they placed their order, Jeff's phone rang. He put it to his ear. "Shawn, what have you got?"

Kayli waited anxiously.

"The food is ordered. We're staying." He put his phone away.

"What did he say?"

"The car came back and cruised through the parking lot. Shawn got out and the car took off before he could catch the plates. He figures the guy won't be back tonight, and said I could take you home." He laughed. "You heard my response." He glanced toward the kitchen. "Maybe Amy can join us on her break."

Chapter 21

"You ready?" Monica asked from the doorway.

Kayli glanced up. Monica had a large bag slung over her shoulder.

"Just shutting down my computer." She paused when she realized that this was the first evening she would be going out simply to have fun. Shawn had brought her back to life. A moment later, she grabbed her purse from a drawer and stood. "Let's go."

"John just called and said he had a minor emergency at work and that we should start without him."

"That's too bad."

"I couldn't tell if he was upset about not joining us or the emergency had him stressed. He hopes to be done in time to have dessert with us."

"Okay. Where are we going?" Kayli stopped beside Monica.

"Oh, *Schaeffer's*. It's the closest restaurant to the park."

After a short walk, they stepped into *Schaeffer's* and to the hostess station. They talked for a minute before a blonde woman approached them.

"I'm sorry to keep you waiting. Two?"

Monica smiled at her. "For dinner, and then a third will join us for dessert."

The woman wrote on a chart and picked up two menus from a stack behind her. "Follow me." She seated them at a booth for four.

The waitress arrived and Kayli ordered chicken cordon

bleu. Monica ordered pot roast.

Monica sipped her water. "I'm so surprised John didn't find someone else to take care of this emergency. Every time I've talked to him, he's mentioned tonight."

"It sounds like he won't miss the concert." It wasn't like he'd be missing a famous performer.

They talked through dinner. "What about dessert?" Monica asked.

"They've got mini desserts here, which is perfect for me."

She caught sight of John approaching their table. He grinned and plopped down beside her. That startled her, and she scooted to give him more room.

"You planned that well," Monica said. "You're just in time for dessert."

Their waitress appeared. "Can I bring anything else?"

John glanced at the women.

"I'll have the mini cheesecake," Kayli said.

"The same for me," Monica said.

John stared at the waitress. "I'll have a regular apple pie with ice cream and coffee."

"I'll be right back with those."

John leaned back and put an arm across the top of the booth. Kayli was glad she'd been sitting straight up. It would seem too intimate for his arm to be so close to her.

"Did you two have a nice dinner?"

Monica smiled. "We did. It's been way too long since Kayli and I have done this. I'm kind of glad you were late."

Sadness swept through Kayli. The last time had been before Max died. They'd gone out to dinner, right from work, every couple months. She could have left Michael with Michelle for an evening or a sleep-over, but she'd never felt an inclination to go. "Me, too." She glanced into Monica's warm eyes. "It was almost like old times."

Her friend reached across the table and squeezed Kayli's arm.

"Here we go." The waitress set small, glass cups in front of the women and a plate in front of John, then placed a full cup beside his plate.

They finished the food, and each paid their share of the bill and stood to go.

John ended up between the women on the walk to the park. A few people had already arrived and sat on folding chairs or blankets near the raised gazebo. They debated where to sit and chose a spot about twenty feet from center stage. Monica pulled out a smooth, cotton blanket and Kayli helped her spread it. John bumped her with his knee when he sat down near her.

Monica pulled a deck of cards from her large bag. "What shall we play?"

She and Max hadn't brought games to play while they waited. She'd lean against him and he'd run his hand through her hair or rub her back as they talked. It was a good memory, but she couldn't dwell on it.

"How about *Peanuts*?" The fast paced game should keep her mind busy.

Monica pulled two more decks of cards from her bag and laughed. "How did I know you'd say that?" She handed one deck to each of them.

They shuffled and laid out their cards. Soon they were slapping cards onto the blanket. They played four rounds before the tune up notes started. The last round was finished and Monica gathered the cards and put them away.

Kayli already faced the gazebo, so she stretched her legs in front of her. Monica and John scooted so they sat on each side of her. He bumped his arm against her shoulder as he moved into place. She hoped he didn't notice that she slid a bit away from him. She liked him, but didn't want him to have any ideas beyond that.

"Hi, everybody." The lead singer introduced himself and the rest of his band. "We'll be singing mostly nineties tunes." He turned to his band and counted down for the first song.

Kayli was pretty amazed at their rendition of *To be with You,* followed by *Can't Help Falling in Love with You.* She pulled her legs up to her chest and wrapped her arms around them, ignoring how John had moved a little closer.

It was dark by the time the band played their last song, *I Will Always Love You.* It made a sour ending for her. A beautiful song, reminding her of the stalker's messages. She shivered.

"It is getting chilling, isn't it," Monica said.

Kayli barely heard the words over the loud applause. She stood, ready to leave now that the mood had been spoiled.

John scrambled up beside her. "How about a drink before we all head home?"

She shook her head. "No. I just want to go home now."

Kayli helped Monica fold the blanket and they strolled to the parking lot beside her work. They reached Kayli's car first and saw her safely locked inside before John walked Monica to her car.

She needed to talk to Shawn. He answered immediately. "Hi, Kayli. How was the concert?"

"Hi, Shawn. It was good, except one song reminded me of the killer."

"I'm sorry. Are you home now?" She felt his soft concern.

"Just got back to my car."

Something rustled. "I'm going to drive over to your place and watch for you. Just to make sure you get in all right."

"You don't have to, but I'd appreciate it. Thanks." She could push the bad thoughts away, knowing Shawn would be there.

~~~

Kayli sighed before opening her car door. Another bar, *Shannon's Favorite*. Before she left the office, Shawn had called to tell her that his brother would replace Scott this evening. She glanced at her phone to see Kyle's picture once more. It should be easier this time. She'd pretend they were meeting to talk about Shawn. Quick steps brought her to the door. She smoothed down her skirt and opened another button on her blouse.

The door was heavier than it looked. She tugged again.

"Let me get that for you." A smooth, deep voice behind her. A hand settled on her shoulder and the other grasped the door, brushing her hand, as he pulled it open.

She glanced up to thank him.

He smiled at her and only briefly glanced lower. "You meeting someone?"

"Um. Working on it." She tried a smile. Hopefully, it looked like one.

His hand squeezed her shoulder as he looked into her eyes. "If I wasn't meeting friends, I'd join you."

She'd been oblivious to men around her, and thought when they started this bar thing, she'd only draw the attention of her stalker. She stepped through the opening and looked around, as he slipped by her and sat at a table with two men and a woman.

This bar was noisier than the last one. Muted light, but not so dim she couldn't see faces. Pool balls cracked in the far left corner. Two pool tables with a light above each. Two men held sticks, one with his arm around a woman.

Booths lined the walls on either side, and tables scattered the center. The bar spanned most of the back wall. Show time. She strutted toward it, only briefly glancing at Shawn as she passed him. She peeked at a table with three men, and one whistled at her. That was the reaction she was supposed to get, but it made her uncomfortable. She did her best to ignore him, and reminded herself that this was for Michael. She spotted two empty stools, and headed toward them. Kyle turned around, and she slowed just a bit, changing direction to the empty stool beside him.

"Is this seat taken?" she asked him.

"It is now." He gave her a sexy grin, and her heart did a little flip. She'd thought they'd looked nothing alike, but that was definitely a Shawn smile. She smiled back and climbed onto the stool. After they introduced themselves, Kyle signaled the bartender and they ordered their drinks.

Kyle leaned toward Kayli, his voice low. "Did Shawn tell you I'm doing this under protest?"

She nodded.

"I think this is a harebrained scheme that's going to get you into trouble."

Kayli pushed back her shoulders and narrowed her eyes. "We need to bring this to a head, and get it over with. I want my son back."

"And if you're not careful, your son might become an orphan."

Kayli's heart twisted. She hadn't thought of it that way. Shawn was nearby and she was sure he could protect her. But there was a chance that something could go wrong.

"Do you have a better plan?" she whispered back.

"No."

"Well, until there *is* a better plan, this is the only thing we can do," Kayli responded. "So, now let's pretend to have a good time."

Kyle exhaled. "All right, let's make my brother jealous, and maybe someone else, too."

He smiled at her and took her hand. He brought it up to his lips and kissed her fingertips.

"That'll do it," Kayli said. "Do you want your brother to beat you up? You should have seen how angry he was with Jeff. It's kind of funny, since it was Shawn's idea."

The bartender set his beer and her sangria in front of them, and they picked up their glasses. Kayli sipped hers and Kyle downed his in a few gulps.

He leaned in. "Did Shawn tell you I decided to become a police officer because he did?"

She shook her head.

"Sunday dinner, he used to talk about the things he did and people he met and helped. I wanted to do that, too. As soon as I got in, he announced he was going to make detective."

"Do you feel like he left you behind?"

He took a swig of his second beer. "Nah. I like what I do. Turned out, he'd been asking good questions at scenes of crimes, piecing evidence together, and helping the detectives. It got him noticed."

Every once in a while Kyle leaned closer to Kayli as if he was telling her a secret.

"Why isn't he a police detective anymore?"

"He had a couple cases where he figured more people died because he wasn't allowed to investigate the way he wanted to."

That must have been one of the reasons Shawn didn't take Al's thoughts on their plan very well. "Tell me about one of them."

"There was this sleazy politician who was being blackmailed. He killed the woman. Shawn thought things didn't add up and started checking this guy's history. His captain made him investigate in a different direction. After someone else Shawn thought was connected to the politician

146

died, he started investigating on his own. He blew it up in that guys face."

"I remember that. Didn't the captain have to resign?"

"Yep." Kayli noticed the pride in Kyle's voice.

He downed his drink and leaned in. "I think it's time to leave."

Kayli nodded. She put her palm on Kyle's cheek, and kissed the other one. "Thank you. It's been nice learning more about Shawn and his family."

Kyle wrapped an arm around her waist, and whispered in her ear as they walked through the bar. "Shawn doesn't look so bad. I guess he trusts me more than Jeff."

Kayli smiled at Shawn. She felt protected with his brother to look after her.

They stopped at Kayli's car and Kyle said, "I'll follow you."

Very soon, they pulled into her driveway. No suspicious cars parked on the street. Kyle met Kayli at her car door and wrapped an arm loosely around her waist as they strolled to the house. Once inside, she locked the door behind them and turned. "Now what? Do you want to play cards? Watch TV? I have board games."

"Board games?"

"Yeah. Monopoly, Yahtzee—"

"Monopoly! I haven't played that since I was a kid. I used to wipe out Shawn."

"Do you want to play?'

"Yeah, let's give it a go."

"I'll be back in a minute. You can go to the dining room." She pointed the way and headed to the hall closet. The shelf at eye level held games. Directly in front of her were Michael's. Candy Land, Dotty Dinosaur, and puzzles. It seemed like forever since they last played together.

A deep breath steadied her. She was doing everything

she could to get him home.

She grabbed the Monopoly and hurried to the dining room and set the game box on the table. "Do you want some wine or soda? I don't have any other alcohol."

"Wine's good."

"Okay. You set up the game, and I'll get the wine."

Kyle organized the property cards when Kayli returned to the dining room with stemware in one hand and an opened bottle of merlot in the other. She set the glasses down, and poured.

She sat down across from Kyle. "Let's go over the rules."

Kyle eyebrows raised. "Everybody knows the rules for Monopoly."

"You'd be amazed at how many different house rules people have." She pulled out the game instructions and started reading off bits and pieces. "And there's no kitty for Free Parking," she said.

"What? Of course there is."

"No. Look." She turned the sheet so Kyle could see and pointed to the appropriate section.

Kyle snatched the paper from her and read a few lines. "You're right! I'm sure it was in another version of the game."

She laughed and took them back from Kyle. "My house, these rules." They reviewed the rest of the rules and started the game. After they'd acquired most of the properties, the game got more tense. Kyle grumbled every time he landed on Free Parking and didn't get money. He grumbled again when he landed on a property where Kayli owned a hotel. He didn't hold in his glee when she landed on his property. In between, they talked and laughed.

Kayli glanced at the wine bottle, surprised it was almost empty. She'd only refilled her glass once. Kyle emptied the bottle into his glass. She felt relaxed and clear headed, but there was no way she'd let him drive home. She caught her bottom lip between her teeth. This could be bad in so many ways, starting with Shawn's reaction.

It didn't take much longer before Kayli won the game, and they packed it back into the box. The last time she'd played was with Max, and she hadn't thought about him during the entire game. It didn't hurt to think about it now.

Kyle checked the time. "I think it's late enough. I should go now." His words slurred slightly.

"Kyle, I think you've had too much to drink to drive home."

He looked at the wine bottle. "I only had half a bottle."

"More than half. And what you had at the bar. Why don't I call you a cab? Or, or you could sleep in the guest room."

"I'm fine." He spun around to leave and caught the table with his hand as he wobbled. "Okay, no sudden moves." He stood still for several seconds, as if waiting for the dizziness to pass. "Maybe you're right."

"Yes, I am." She grabbed his arm and guided him up the stairs. "That's the bathroom." She pointed. "Here's the room you're staying in." She pushed him inside. "See you in the morning."

She padded to her bedroom, and locked the door. She liked Shawn's brother, but was concerned that he'd drunk so much when he should have been on alert.

~~~

Kayli was awakened by her phone ringing. She glanced at the clock. *Who calls at six o'clock on a Saturday morning? Oh, that's right. Shawn.* She'd had too few hours of sleep, so put the pillow over her head. The ringing stopped, and picked up again.

She verified the caller ID. "Good morning, Shawn. Did you have to wake me?"

"Kayli, what happened last night? I haven't been able to reach Kyle."

"Let's see. We came back here, played Monopoly, and he drank too much. I couldn't let him drive home drunk, so I stuck him in the guest room. Maybe you should talk to him about his drinking."

"He got drunk? He's supposed to protect you!" She pulled the phone from her ear. He didn't have to yell at her.

" Was I supposed to take the bottle away? We're behind locked doors, with an alarm system, just like I am every night. I think I'm safe."

"But you might not have been safe from Kyle." he grumbled. "He doesn't normally drink that much, and he knew he was on a job."

"I locked my bedroom door. It's over now. I'm going back to sleep. Bye, Shawn." Kayli shut off the phone and set it on the nightstand. She lay back down. It was kind of cute how Shawn was so jealous, even knowing it was pretend attention. Of course, they'd started as pretend, too. Soon, this would be over. The events of the last few weeks ran through her head, and she couldn't relax enough to go back to sleep. Might as well get up. Maybe she could sneak in a Skype call with Michael.

Chapter 22

When Kyle came downstairs, Kayli was finishing the last of her orange juice, an empty plate in front of her.

"Morning, Kyle. How are you feeling?"

"I've got a headache, but I've had worse mornings."

"There's some ibuprofen in that cabinet." She pointed to one beside the refrigerator. "There's a plate of French toast and bacon in the oven for you. I'm sure your nose can find the coffee."

"Thanks, Kayli. You're a life saver."

The oven door opened, and she said, "Use a pot holder."

Kyle sat down across from her, and set his plate on the blue linen placemat. She let him eat half his food before she spoke. "Okay, tell me what happened last night."

"I drank too much."

"Obviously. But why?" It couldn't be his normal behavior or Shawn wouldn't have let him near her.

He didn't answer.

She covered his hand. "Kyle, you're holding down a strenuous job. That can't be how much you usually drink. There's something going on."

He sighed. "You're right. My girlfriend broke up with me two days ago. You being all dewy-eyed over Shawn made me jealous."

She was dewy-eyed? Just thinking about Shawn made her heart race, so maybe it was true.

"There you go again!"

"Sorry. So why did she break up with you?"

"I don't want to talk about it." He viciously cut a piece of French toast.

"Fine. But ask yourself this, is it something you can fix or change to get her back? And do you love her enough to do it? That's all I'm going to say about it." She studied him as he finished eating. He didn't meet her eyes or say anything, so maybe he was thinking about her advice.

He took his dishes to the kitchen and leaned against the counter. "Kayli, thanks for breakfast. Sorry I drank too much last night."

"It's fine. No harm done, but you should probably leave now."

"Yeah. I've got stuff to do." He cocked his head. "Maybe stop by my ex's."

She led him to the door and followed him down her walk. He stopped and swore. She stepped around him and gasped at the sight of his car. "Oh, Kyle! I can't believe he did this again."

He fisted his hands and grimaced.

Kyle's windshield was smashed, a white envelope sat in the midst of the shards. Kayli wrapped her arms around herself and glanced around. He was probably gone, but she felt exposed near the damaged car.

She steeled herself, ran up to the car and checked both sides. "Well, at least he didn't slash your tires like Shawn's."

Through tight lips, Kyle said, "Shawn didn't tell me about this risk." He grabbed her hand. "Let's get back inside." He slammed and locked the door behind them.

"Nothing happened to Jeff's car." She headed toward the kitchen for her phone and glanced over her shoulder. "I have to call Al."

She returned to find Kyle pacing. "Al doesn't live far from here, so he shouldn't be long. Do you want to check the video while we're waiting?"

Kyle nodded and followed her to the alarm system. She sped backwards through the video until a man came into view and disappeared again. She stopped the rewind and continued in regular time.

There he was. The man who'd destroyed her life. "Three-forty-five. If you'd left when you were supposed to, this wouldn't have happened."

"Ski mask and gloves," he said. "Seems to know what he's doing. I bet he knows you've got the camera out there."

Kyle hit rewind. "Let me see that again." He played through in slow motion.

The man came off the street and glanced around. He stopped in front of the driver's door of Kyle's car and lifted a tire iron that appeared to be padded, and started smashing in the windshield. Then he went to the other side and did the same. He pulled an envelope out of his pocket and stuck it under the wiper, then walked away.

He gave a low whistle. "Wow. There's a lot of anger in him. I'm glad he didn't come at me like that. But not so angry that he's making mistakes. Let's play it again. Maybe you'll recognize the way he moves."

Once more they watched the scene. Each step, turn of his head, movement of his arms. Nothing seemed familiar.

A car stopped outside and they went to the door as Al stepped from his car. "What are you doing here, Kyle?"

"I was Kayli's date last night."

Al looked at Kayli. "You're still doing that? I told Shawn you shouldn't. By the way, where is he?"

She used air quotes. "We broke up." She dropped her arms. "He can't be here. Al, we watched the video. There's no sense checking for fingerprints. He wore gloves, and he didn't touch anything."

"All right. I'll have security send me the video anyway. Now let's see what he has to say." He put on latex gloves, plucked the envelope from the windshield, pulled out the sheet of paper, and flattened it on the car hood. They all leaned in to read it.

Enough of this.
Your love belongs to me.
Only me!

Al glanced at Kayli. "You and Shawn are playing with fire here."

Ice skittered down her spine. "It doesn't go away if we do nothing."

"I can have a police car escort you to work and home."

It was tempting, but the killer would probably back off, and she'd never be able to safely bring Michael home. "I think we have to keep doing what we're doing."

"Have it your way." He pulled a bag out of his pocket and carefully put the letter and envelope into it. "I'll let you know if anything comes up." He stalked back to his car.

Kayli turned to Kyle. "Do you want to have your car towed or do you want the windshield people to come here and replace it?" She hoped he chose to have it done in her driveway so she wouldn't have to be home alone.

~~~

Kayli sat with Kyle in the living room, getting to know him. She liked Shawn's brother. Her stomach growled and she offered to make sandwiches. They ate in the kitchen. The windshield people arrived as they cleared lunch dishes. They moved their conversation back to the living room, until a knock on the door let them know the job was done.

Kayli followed Kyle to the door. They inspected the new windshield, and the workers left.

Kyle made shooing motions. "Back inside before I leave."

"Okay. I enjoyed your visit." She kissed his cheek and headed into the house, locking the door. Kyle's car engine roared to life and he drove away.

Kayli called Shawn.

"Hi, Shawn. Kyle just left."

"Just left? It's the middle of the afternoon."

"It got a little busy here with Al and the windshield people."

"What? What happened, Kayli?"

"We discovered this morning that Kyle's windshield had been smashed and the stalker left a note. Fortunately, his tires weren't slashed."

"I'm coming over."

"Shawn, no. We've put too much into this to spoil our plan now." They had to keep doing this for Michael. She'd already done scary things. She could do this. "The alarm is set. I'm safe in the house."

Shawn let his breath out. "All right. What did the note say?"

She told him.

"Kayli, be really careful. Get an escort to your car at night. It sounds like he's approaching his limit."

Her stomach churned, and she wrapped an arm around her middle. "I'll be even more careful. I wish you could be the one to escort me, but I know you can't."

"Since this happened, we'll assume that the guy you picked up wouldn't want to have another date with you, so we'll set up another bar date for Friday."

Kayli sighed. "Okay. I hope this is over soon."

"Me, too. I'll talk to you tomorrow."

The killer didn't just sit in his car and watch. Twice he'd damaged cars in her driveway. One night he could wait in the bushes near her door when she came home from work. She'd assumed he only came by late at night. That might not be the case.

Chapter 23

Kayli pulled into the parking lot of another bar, *Fired Up*, checked the time on the dash clock, and sighed. Michael needed to be home with her and she wanted to spend real time with Shawn. Not just talk to him on the phone or walk past him in a bar.

She touched the circle of diamonds at her throat, and let it center her. She was doing this for Max and Michael. She pushed her door open, and stood beside the car, looked down at her outfit. The blue skirt was much shorter than she was comfortable with. It had been in the back of her closet, stuck there probably years ago. Tugging it down made no difference in its length.

She straightened her shoulders and let each step put her more into the pickup mode. She pushed the door open. This bar wasn't as loud as the last. Music played, but she didn't recognize the sultry voice or slow beat. Her target, a pair of empty seats at the bar. She passed Shawn, tucked into a corner of a booth halfway there, and gave him a small smile as his gaze traveled from her head to her feet. They might have lingered at her hemline. His was the one set of eyes she didn't mind looking at her like that.

She felt more uncomfortable tonight than the other nights. All eyes seemed to be on her. The bartender watched her approach, and she swallowed a lump. There weren't enough other women in the bar, which didn't help her feel better. She had no idea why Shawn would have chosen this place.

She climbed onto a stool and the bartender stepped in front of her. He leaned on an elbow. "What can I get ya', darlin'?"

She wondered if he called all women darling, or if he was hitting on her. If she really was looking to pick up a guy, she'd have a quick comeback, but instead, she placed her order. She glanced down the bar where several men, some standing, conversed. On her right, a woman sat between two men. They laughed at something said by the man closer to her. Past them, a lone man sat, but he wasn't Scott.

The bartender set her glass in front of her and Kayli thanked him.

"I haven't seen you here before. I hope you'll become a regular."

"It's not what I'm used to."

He leaned closer. She got the idea he wished the bar wasn't between them.

"I didn't think so. You're too classy for this place."

"Hey, Alex!"

The bartender glanced to the end and nodded. He sighed. "Sorry. Gotta get back to work."

She looked for Scott and still didn't see him. Someone brushed her shoulder as he took the seat on her left.

"John!" To be found like this by someone she knew was almost embarrassing. "I didn't expect you to be here. Is this a regular place for you?" She didn't know what to do. Scott could arrive any minute. Maybe she should tell John she had a blind date.

"I come in occasionally. It's surprising to find you here alone, and especially sitting at the bar."

He didn't smile like he usually did when they saw each other. He probably disapproved of her being there. She hadn't seen him without Monica before, and wondered what her secretary would have to say on Monday, after her brother told her about seeing Kayli. He probably wasn't sure how to behave with her like this. Or maybe he had a bad day. The comradery she'd felt with Monica and John together was absent.

"Oh, I, um, needed to get out." The best thing to do was chat with him. It wasn't a good idea to tell him her real reason for being there. They'd deal with the situation when Scott showed up.

~~~

Shawn didn't take his eyes off Kayli and the man beside her. He'd come in minutes after Kayli and made a beeline for her. The same man who'd watched her so intently at the other two bars. He hated doing it, but he had to let it play out a bit longer. Each moment deepened his fear for her. They needed the man to make some kind of move to pin this on him.

Kayli didn't seem distressed, what little he could see of her profile and body language. She probably didn't realize yet that this was the killer.

Shawn caught sight of Scott, and hissed. "Scott." He nodded to the bench across from him.

Scott sat. "Sorry I'm late. What's up?"

"That's him," Shawn said in a low voice.

Scott carefully looked over his shoulder. "Sitting with Kayli?"

"Yeah. I've seen him twice before, watching her. Since you were late, it gave him a chance to move in on her."

Scott gave a quick glance at the bar. "How do you want to proceed?"

"Let's just watch for now." It took everything he had to sit and watch a killer talk to the woman he loved.

~~~

159

Kayli finished her drink and John ordered her another and one for himself.

The bartender, Alex, set hers in front of her and raised an eyebrow. She shrugged the shoulder away from John. It was nice that he was concerned for her. He gave a slight nod and turned away.

Kayli sipped. It tasted weaker than the last one. The bartender really was concerned, and she appreciated it.

Scott should have been here by now. John was spoiling the chances of catching the killer.

He took a long drink of his beer and set it down. "There's a play at the cultural center that's been getting good reviews. Do you want to go with me?" He seemed so eager, leaning a little towards her.

Now what? His sister would have told him that she'd broken up with Shawn, but she didn't want to go on a real date with anyone else.

"Monica was telling me about it," Kayli said. "The three of us should go this week."

John's lips tightened into a straight line. Then he relaxed them and smiled at her. "Kayli, I meant just you and me."

"Oh, John. I don't know." She'd always thought of him as Monica's brother, never realizing he might have had more of an interest in her.

John touched her arm, slid his palm down to her hand and wrapped his fingers around it. He rubbed his thumb across her knuckles.

Kayli's insides cramped. She'd been nervous when Jeff had touched her, but it was nothing like this fear. She'd never felt it around John before, but something wasn't right. He was different tonight—as tense as she was and trying not to show it.

Strong, intense emotion bubbled under his surface, nothing like the John she was used to. Maybe something else disturbed him. He couldn't be her stalker.

His smile sent a shiver through her.

He leaned in closer. "Maybe we should just skip right to the end of this little meeting, and go to your house now."

Her heart stopped beating for several seconds, and then it raced. "John, what are you saying?" He was Monica's brother. The three of them had gone out together. He couldn't be this other person. She'd considered him a friend. John wouldn't have killed Max or tried to kill Michael. She would have picked up on it before.

John's hand tightened on hers. It didn't hurt, but her hand was trapped. "You put out for strangers. Just think how much better it will be with me."

Her blood turned to ice. She'd never thought about how they'd catch the killer, but it would never have been like this. It should have been a stranger.

"John, I don't want to do this." She tried to tug her hand and he squeezed it until her fingers crushed together.

With his other hand, he touched her cheek. Kayli flinched, and John frowned. "Kayli, you came here to pick up a man." He began in a reasonable voice, but then his words turned harsh. "I'm your only choice. Now and forever."

She tried to slow down her breathing and think. Nothing came to her, except that this man, who she thought she knew, had killed Max. A killer held her hand.

John reached into his jacket pocket, and pulled out a switchblade. With a flick of his thumb, a sharp blade flashed open. He held it low, close to his body. Nobody would have noticed. It was probably the same knife he'd used on Shawn's tires, and just as easy to use on her. Shawn was close. He'd rescue her.

John's eyes were still on her face. In a soft voice, he said, "Kayli, I love you. I never meant it to be this way. I was going to be so gentle with you. Ease you out of your sorrow.

Make you fall in love with me." His voice hardened. "But you never really noticed me. I was only Monica's brother to you."

Kayli stiffened to stop the full body tremble. She'd never thought out what would happen when the killer confronted her. He was a faceless man she'd never met.

John had always been friendly and normal. Her heart pounded so loud he must hear it. She needed to calm down. Find a way to make him see reason. "John, I never knew. Let's just back up, and take it slow."

"It's too late for that. We're leaving. Now." He slid off his stool and pulled Kayli down in front of him.

Her legs were too rubbery to hold her and she grabbed the stool to steady herself. Maybe Kyle was right and Michael would become an orphan tonight. No! It wasn't over yet. Shawn wouldn't let that happen.

John grabbed her left hand, and settled it with his over her stomach. They probably looked like a cozy couple. "We're going to walk to your car, and you'll drive us home. Don't try anything foolish." He pushed the knife into her side just enough to prick her but not cause any real pain.

She nodded.

"I don't want to hurt you." She could almost believe the pain in his voice. John gave her a nudge. "Let's go."

His hip bumped hers as they stepped forward together. Every few paces, the knife pricked her side. If he stumbled, she'd probably die.

They were coming up on Shawn's table. "Why do you want to go to my house?"

John's arm tightened around her. "That's where you take them all, isn't it? I want you to be comfortable, Kayli."

She suppressed a shiver. He was a scary mix of sane and crazy.

She briefly met Shawn's eyes, and hoped he'd heard.

162

She didn't know how he'd rescue her without one of them getting seriously hurt.

They reached the passenger side of her Camry. He fished into her purse, brought out the keys, clicked the button to unlock the door, and opened it. "Get inside."

She sat and tried to pull the door between them, and John yanked it open. It wouldn't have done her much good anyway, since he had the keys.

"Put your feet over the console and scoot to the driver's seat."

Easier said than done in this stupid skirt that she'd never wear again. Once over the console, she lunged for the door handle and pushed. He grabbed her arm and pulled her back into the seat.

"Try that again and I'll cut you." He took her chin between his thumb and forefinger and turned her head. "Kayli, I don't want to hurt you."

She jerked back. His whipsaw emotions were scarier than just the anger. Her heart hammered, but wasn't as loud as the breaths rasping in and out of her lungs. She tugged her miniscule skirt down, anything to delay what came next.

He jammed the key in the ignition and started the car, then put his revolting hand on her thigh.

"Drive."

~~~

Shawn shook with rage. He'd seen the terror on Kayli's face. That bastard wouldn't get a chance to take her back to her house. He couldn't risk the killer shooting one of the customers, so it would end in the parking lot.

Scott put his hand on Shawn's arm. "Calm down, man. You won't do her any good like that."

"Did you see how he was holding his right arm? He's got

a weapon on her." She could die because he screwed up. He needed to save her, no matter if that cost his life.

He kept his eyes on their retreating backs, and scooted to the edge of the booth. "As soon as they hit the door, we're after them."

"Let's do it," Scott said.

Shawn sprung up and stumbled into a man and woman. The man shoved him. "Watch what you're doing."

"Sorry." Shawn untangled himself from the couple.

The man grabbed Shawn's arm and got in his face. "Are you trying to feel up my woman?"

They were losing precious seconds. His heart pounded faster. "No. I have to get out of here. Now."

Scott put a hand on the man's shoulder. "He's got an emergency."

The man glared at Shawn for too many seconds, and finally pushed back from him.

They'd lost a frustrating amount of time. Shawn flung the door open and rushed outside, to watch Kayli's car exiting the lot. "No!"

Scott squeezed his shoulder. "It's not over yet."

It wasn't, but it was a whole lot more dangerous for Kayli. "I'll beat them to Kayli's house, and jump him when they walk in. You follow the car in case they go somewhere else."

They raced to their cars.

Shawn dialed Al's number.

"Al Barnes."

"Al. It's Shawn. The killer has Kayli. I think they're going to her house. Meet me there. No sirens. If you get there before they do, I don't want him to take off somewhere else with her." He hung up before Al could respond.

As he broke speed limits and ran red lights, he called himself every name he could think of for allowing this to happen to Kayli. She willingly followed his plan, believing he could protect her. And he'd allowed her to fall into the hands of a killer. He hit his hand on the steering wheel. She had to be okay. He'd give his own life if it meant that he could save her.

Shawn parked on the street, three doors past Kayli's and sprinted back to her house. He let himself in with the key he'd never given back and reset the security system. It would give another notification to the police when the killer entered.

He pushed the sheer beside the door partially open so he'd have a view of the walk, then paced in the dark.

They might not come here. What if Scott lost them? The killer could take her to his place or some secluded spot. She might be raped or die while he waited in her living room. Unwanted scenes of Kayli struggling against a killer played in his head. He pushed them away. He needed to stay strong and be ready.

Headlights flashed across the window as a car pulled into the driveway. Relief washed with a new tension filled him. His heart thudded loud in his ears as he watched their approach through the window, Kayli in the lead. She would survive this no matter what he had to do.

The killer reached around her, the key turned in the lock, and then the door opened.

Shawn waited, ready to spring. Seconds ticked by.

"Get in." The voice of the killer.

Kayli lurched in. The man had probably pushed her.

It gave Shawn some space. He dove between her and the kidnapper. She hit the floor, and her breath expelled from her lungs behind him.

"Shawn! He's got a knife!"

Shawn dodged a jab. "Kayli, lock yourself in the bathroom, then call 911."

She scrambled up and footsteps sped away. The

165

bathroom door slammed shut.

Calm enveloped him. Kayli was okay and he'd make sure she stayed that way. Now it was time for Shawn to end this.

The guy jabbed the knife at Shawn's torso and he leaped back. At these close quarters, his gun was a worse weapon than the knife, and he wanted both hands free to disable the man.

Shawn tried to grab the killer's arm, and got a scratch. He hoped it was a scratch. He kicked at the hand, but hit air. As the man lunged, Shawn caught the knife arm and pushed it over their heads. The killer's breath rasped in Shawn's ear. With all the force the man put into pushing, Shawn couldn't lift his foot to knock the guy's leg out, or he'd be the one on the floor.

"I really don't want to dance with you," Shawn grunted.

"Give me a minute and you'll be sitting out your life, and Kayli will be dancing with me."

No way would this man touch Kayli again.

The killer pushed against Shawn's chest and jumped back, yanking his wrist free. Shawn kick at the knife arm. He caught a glimpse of Scott, finally. The killer pulled his arm back, and Scott grabbed the guy's wrist, wrenching it up behind his back. Scott plucked the knife from his fingers and tossed it across the room. Then he slammed the killer to the floor, and put his knee into the man's spine.

"You're a life saver, but you could have come in sooner."

Scott grinned. "I was giving you a chance to be the hero."

"Yeah, I have to brush up on my self-defense-against-knives training."

"I'm going to zip tie him," Scott said. "Why don't you check on Kayli?"

Shawn approached the bathroom door and knocked. "Kayli, it's Shawn. You can come out now."

The lock turned, and the door flew open. Tears streaked Kayli's face, and her lips trembled. She paused a moment before throwing herself into his arms. "I was so scared. I was afraid he'd kill you."

Shawn sucked in a breath, and Kayli pulled back.

"Are you okay?" She flipped on the hall light and glanced down. "You're bleeding!"

She ripped his shirt open. A five-inch cut, smooth and deep, crossed his ribs. He hadn't felt it until she hugged him.

Kayli dragged him to the kitchen. She yanked open a kitchen drawer and snatched up two dish towels, pressing them over the wound.

He put his hands over hers. "I'll hold it."

"But—"

He put his other arm around her waist and snugged her to his side, his cheek on her head. "I was so worried about you. I'm sorry I put you through all this."

She wrapped one arm around Shawn and pulled him closer.

"Let's go see how Scott is doing," Shawn said.

Kayli started to shake. "I can't go out there. I don't want to see John."

Shawn pulled back and stared at her. "John? You know him?"

She nodded. "He's Monica's brother." She put her head on Shawn's chest. "I don't know what she'll do when she finds out."

Even when she'd come so close to being hurt, she thought of someone else's welfare.

Shawn pulled her closer. "It's Stewart?"

She nodded against his chest.

"Why don't I walk you to your office? You can stay in

there while we take care of this. If Al needs to talk to you, I'll bring him back." He could just make out sirens in the distance. That wouldn't be Al.

They entered her office, and he led her to her overstuffed chair, picked up a throw and tucked it around her as best as he could with one hand. He leaned down and kissed her forehead. Pain shot through his ribs, but it was worth it. "I'll be back as soon as I can."

Her eyes were on the bloody towel. "When it's all over, we're taking you to the hospital for stitches."

"Yeah." It would need stitches, and the pain was intense, but no way was he telling her that.

"Shawn, does it hurt a lot? Here you are taking care of me and you're the one who's injured."

"It's not so bad when I don't think about it. Kayli, I'm more concerned about your reaction to everything that's happened. But, we'll deal with that after everybody's cleared out." He forced himself to leave her.

Shawn joined Scott near the front door. He stood over John, who was still on his face on the floor.

"So, Scott, do you always carry zip ties on a date?" Shawn forced a grin. Kayli was fine. He could relax.

Scott glared. "Only when there's a possibility of a psycho joining us."

"I'm not a psycho," John said from the floor. "You'll see that Kayli's mine as soon as you let me talk to her."

Scott kicked him in the ribs. "Shut up."

"You're lucky I didn't see that." Al said as he hurried through the open door.

"See what? Nothing to see, but this creep." Scott dropped a foot on John's back, then shook Al's hand.

Al frowned and nodded at the floor. "So, who have we here?"

Shawn glared at the man on the floor. "This is John

Stewart. Kayli's secretary's brother."

Al's eyebrows hiked up. "That was close to home."

Sirens blared into the room.

Al leaned over. "Scott, can you help me get this scum to his feet?"

Once John was standing, Al read his rights as he led him outside, with Scott following.

"You have to let me talk to Kayli. She'll explain how much I love her. She needs me. Only me."

Chapter 24

Al returned and pointed at Shawn's ribs. "How bad is that?"

Shawn tipped the towel away and fresh blood seeped out of the cut. With the pressure off, a new surge of pain sliced through him.

"Yeah, better get that stitched soon. Let's see if we can wrap this up ASAP. Where's Kayli?"

"In her office." Shawn pointed, leading Al and Scott down the hall. He stopped in the doorway when he saw Kayli's head leaning back against the cushion. He whispered, "She's asleep."

"Are you kidding?" She gave Shawn a pained stare. "I was trying to get myself to relax. I have a headache."

Shawn sat on the arm of her chair. Her arm snaked out from under the throw and Shawn held her hand.

Scott and Al pulled up chairs. Al spoke first. "Kayli, let's start with you. Where were you when this guy showed up?"

"I was sitting at the bar at Kelly's Pub, waiting for Scott."

"I was late," Scott interjected.

"Then John sat down beside me."

Her hand trembled and Shawn gave it a squeeze. He wished he could sweep her up into his arms, but one hand had to hold the towel to his ribs.

"Did you know him?" Al asked.

"Yes. He's my secretary's brother." She described their conversation. "I didn't know he was the killer until he got angry when I refused to go out with him. So we walked out of the bar with the knife at my back."

"I'm sorry, Kayli," Shawn said. She looked up at him. The pain in her eyes tore at him. Al had been right. They'd played with fire and gotten burned.

She turned to Al. "I tried to talk him out of it after we got in my car, but he just told me to shut up."

"Let me take it from here," Shawn said, and explained his race to the house and Scott's following the car.

He turned to Kayli. "I'm sorry for pushing you to the floor."

"You saved my life, Shawn." Love glowed in her eyes.

He gave her hand a squeeze and turned back to Al. "I sent Kayli to lock herself in the bathroom and wrestled with the guy. Then Scott came in and took him down."

"All right." Al studied each of them and shook his head. "This could have turned out so much worse. We're good for now." He stood. "I want the three of you to come to the station tomorrow and give your statements. And you," he pointed at Shawn, "better get to the hospital."

They all headed to the front door. Al and Scott left. Kayli picked up her purse from the floor. "Let's go."

Shawn shook his head. "You're not going anywhere."

"I'm taking you to the hospital. You need to keep pressure on that, so you can't drive yourself."

"I can—"Kayli's determination expression convinced him he'd have to relent. "Okay. You can drive."

~~~

Two and a half hours later, Shawn opened his eyes as Kayli pulled back into her driveway. It was nearly morning, and he was exhausted. Without her arm around him, he might not have made it into the house. And then there were the

171

stairs to climb.

Once the door was locked and the security system engaged, she gave him a gentle hug. "It scared me when the doctor said that two inches lower and that knife would have cut deep into your intestines."

Shawn kissed the top of her head. Not something he wanted to think about. "But it didn't. I only needed a few stitches."

"A few! It was twenty-three." She yawned. "I'm exhausted. Let's go to bed."

His heart rate sped up. He wasn't sure exactly what Kayli meant. She stepped free and pulled his hand as she headed to the stairs.

In front of her door, he wrapped his arms around her and kissed her. He'd let her decide what was going to happen, but a little nudge wouldn't hurt.

She looked up at him. "The guest room."

Shawn nodded and gave her one more kiss. "All right. I'll see you in the morning." He turned.

Kayli circled her arm around his waist. "We'll sleep there." Shawn stopped and looked down at her with surprise. She waved behind her. "That was my room with Max. I want somewhere that's just ours."

Shawn gave her a sexy smile and kissed her again. They entered the guest room, and he pulled off his ruined shirt, dropping it on the floor. It could go in the trash tomorrow. He unbuckled his belt, feeling Kayli's eyes on him. "I hope it won't disappoint you, but between these fresh stitches and the long night, I'm exhausted. Do you mind if I just hold you until we fall asleep?"

She smiled. "I can't think of a better place to be than in your arms."

She undid her skirt and it slid to the floor. She stepped out of it. His eyes were riveted to her silky, black bikinis. Her fingers unbuttoned her shirt, but held the edges together. A diamond necklace gleamed above her hands. She bit her lip. Sexy and nervous.

"You can go put on some night clothes, if you want. I'll leave on my briefs." He could slip into bed while she was gone.

She pulled in a long breath, and threw back the shirt flaps, letting it slip down her body.

He dragged his eyes back to her face. If he hadn't already told her he was just going to sleep, he'd be very tempted to make love to her. A quickly indrawn breath and the stab of pain reminded him of the other reason he couldn't. He touched her face. "You don't have to take off any more."

His words seemed to push her, but that wasn't his intent.

She reached behind her. "I can't sleep in my bra." The offending article loosened and dropped to the floor at her feet.

He held his breath. He couldn't touch those beautiful peaks, or he wouldn't stop until he tore stitches.

The loss of her bra seemed to prompt her to hurry. She peeled off her panties and dove under the covers.

He pulled his wallet from his pocket, set it on the nightstand, and removed his remaining clothing. He joined her in the bed, groaning with the sharp pain at the movement. Lying on his right side, he pulled her close and kissed her. "Now turn your back to me." She did as he asked and he wrapped an arm around her. "You feel perfect, Kayli. Just don't elbow me in the ribs."

"Shawn!"

He chuckled and kissed her behind the ear. Very soon they both slept.

Chapter 25

Kayli woke slowly, feeling totally relaxed. It had been months since she'd felt this good in the morning. Her head rested on Shawn's shoulder, and she moved it so her cheek rubbed it. One hand rested on his stomach. A quick check ensured her it didn't cover his bandage. Shawn's arm circled her back, and his hand lightly gripped her hip. She didn't move. It felt too good to want to change anything.

"Good morning, Kayli."

She looked up at him. "Morning. Have you been awake long?"

"About a half hour." She raised her eyebrows and he smiled. "It felt too good holding you like this to move."

"That's what I was thinking when I woke up. But now that we're both awake..." She slid up a few inches and kissed him. Shawn returned the kiss, then pulled back.

"You seem different."

Kayli stiffened. "A good different or a bad different?"

"Oh, definitely good."

Kayli exhaled. "It's because I let go of Max." She gazed at him. He watched her, saying nothing. "Before, when I was with you, in my heart, I felt like I was cheating on Max. In my head, I knew it was crazy. Then, the Sunday we had that long talk on the phone, I finally felt able to get rid of Max's clothes."

Shawn's head jerked back, and Kayli lowered her eyes. Maybe it hadn't been a good idea to tell him. She'd kept those clothes for three years. He probably thought she was crazy.

Shawn put a finger under her chin and raised it. He kissed her. "I'm glad I somehow helped you let go."

It was her turn to be surprised. "I was sad, but I felt good about giving his clothes away. Then I found the jacket Max had worn…that last day. It got left in the car. When I was folding it, I felt a lump in the pocket." Kayli stared at her toes wiggling under the blanket. The pain she'd experienced on finding the gift had become a dull ache. "It was my birthday present." She had accepted Max's death, but tears still prickled her eyes.

Shawn's arm tightened around her. She lifted the necklace she still wore. "He said that the circle of diamonds represented us surrounding Michael with our love." She was getting Michael back. Even with the remembrance of this last gift, her heart soared.

Kayli started to pull away and Shawn frowned. She leaned forward and kissed him. "I have to get something. I'll be right back."

~~~

Shawn watched her walk across the room, admiring every movement. She disappeared out the door. He wasn't sure what to think. Kayli had pulled away, but then kissed him before leaving. His thoughts were in turmoil. He knew how much she'd loved her husband. She'd pined for him for years. Was she really ready to let go?

Kayli came back into the room, carrying a small card. She slipped under the covers, but remained sitting, pressed against Shawn's side. She handed him the card. "This was with the necklace." She handed it to him.

He studied her before looking at the card. Her eyes shimmered like she almost had tears. He opened the card and

175

read it.

Happy Birthday, Kayli. I cherish every moment I spend with you. Let's celebrate each day together as if there is no tomorrow.

Love, Max

Kayli was supposed to have received this on the day Max died. For them, there was no tomorrow before she'd even seen it. He couldn't imagine how hard it had been for her to read this.

"Kayli, I'm so sorry." He ran his fingers down the side of her cheek. She caught his hand and kissed it.

She blinked back the tears that threatened. "Shawn, I needed you to see it." She took the card from him and set it on the nightstand. She took off the necklace and placed it on the card, then kissed him and straightened back up.

"A small part of my heart will always love Max." Shawn squeezed her hand. "But the rest of it belongs to you and Michael. I don't want to live in a self-created cage anymore. I love you and I want to celebrate with you."

He pulled Kayli's head down for a kiss. "I love you, Kayli. When I realized last night that I could lose you, it drove me crazy. I want to spend the rest of my life with you and Michael. Marry me."

She stretched out on her side and leaned across him. An inch from his mouth she gave him the answer he wanted. "Yes." She kissed him.

He didn't expect the burst of happiness that rushed through him. "I want to make love to you, but—" He waved a hand to his side. "—I'm a wounded man. Want to help me out?"

She grinned and straddled him.

"One more thing. Can you grab my wallet?" He nodded toward the nightstand.

She came up on her knees and snagged it, holding it

above her head. "Why? You're not paying me, are you?"

He smiled widely. "You paid me. Remember? No. I've got a couple of condoms in there."

"Oh." She shoved it into his hand. "I used to be on birth control."

Which is why she hadn't thought of protection. He fished the packages out and dropped his wallet to the floor. He crooked a finger. "Now, come on down here."

She eased down on his uninjured side, one sweet breast pressed into his chest, the other free for him to caress. Her right thigh was cradled between his legs, exerting just the right pressure against his balls.

His right arm circle her back, so she wouldn't slide off him. He kissed her the way he'd been dreaming of for weeks, as his left hand touched and teased her breast. His full fantasy would have to wait for his cut to heal, but this was going to be every bit as good. No. Better.

He slid his hand lower, through her curls and into her folds. She moaned and tangled her fingers in his hair, then rested her forehead against his cheek as ragged breaths shook her. Three years since her last time. He needed to make sure she was ready. He slipped a finger inside her as his thumb worked her. She squirmed and he held her tighter. Her thigh rubbed his balls. He wouldn't last long once he was inside her.

She stiffened. "Shawn!" Ripples flowed through her. She threw back her head and he kissed her neck. "I can't believe I forgot how good it was."

His perfect woman. "We're not done yet, sweetheart. Unless you want to be."

She pushed up and looked around. "Where's the condom?"

He felt around and wrapped his fingers around it. "Here. Do you know how to use it?"

She gave him a disdainful glare. "Of course, I do."

His chuckle turned to a groan as her fingers touched him and rolled it on. He steadied her, his hands on her shoulders, as she straddled him. Her eyes glowed with love. He wondered if she saw the same in his.

He couldn't resist touching her breasts again. He squeezed her nipples and she closed her eyes. Then she lowered herself, taking him into her, and they hissed in unison. It took everything in him not to surge up into her, to let her determine how quickly he filled her.

Once fully seated, she leaned forward. He lifted his head, but a twinge in his side stopped him. With a hand on each of his shoulders, she lifted and dropped. Three more times before he had to take control. His hands grasped her hips and he surged up. Pain took him by surprise and he dropped back down with a groan.

"Shawn."

"No. It's all right."

He lifted her hips and let her slide back. The pain was forgotten. They worked together as she moved over him. He was so close, but wanted to make sure she came with him. He shifted one hand to her center. She plunged faster, then her climax brought him with her. She slumped forward and he turned her to his good side.

He caressed her back as they recovered. "I love you, Kayli." He kissed her temple. This was where they belonged. Together.

Chapter 26

Shawn loaded their breakfast dishes into the dishwasher. "Kayli, it's time to go see Al."

She nodded. "I'm not looking forward to going through all that again."

"I know, but look at how far you've come."

She gave him a quick kiss. "I couldn't have done it without you."

He wrapped his arms around her. "After we see Al, let's pick up Michael."

She held him tight. "It'll be so good to have him back."

At the security panel, Shawn punched in the code. He started to head to the front door when Kayli grabbed his arm. "Wait. Since we're celebrating today," she swung the door to the garage open, "let's take the Mustang."

He glanced into the garage to find an empty first bay. He looked at her in surprise. "The Subaru is gone."

She nodded. "The day after I emptied the closet, I had my mechanic pick it up. He ended up buying it on the spot for his wife. Then he came back, towed the Mustang and serviced it. So, it's ready to drive." She pulled the keys out of her purse and held them out to Shawn.

"You should drive it the first time," he said.

Kayli bit her lip. "I don't know how to drive a stick."

Shawn chuckled and took the keys. "We'll have to remedy that real soon." He kissed her. Kayli hit the button to open the garage door and together they removed the cover.

After they got into the car, Shawn inspected the interior.

The leather practically glowed, chrome sparkled. "Wow."

"My mechanic said his wife was so excited to get the Subaru, she detailed it for me."

Shawn unclipped the convertible top and lowered it.

Kayli laughed. "You look like you just got the present you've always dreamed about."

He cradled her head with his hand, and pulled her toward him. He kissed her until thought of anything else fled.

"You are the present I've dreamed about. This," he gestured around them, "is just icing on the cake."

They put the top back up when they parked at the police station and walked hand-in-hand inside. They were directed back to Al's office. Al looked up and smiled when they stepped in.

"Kayli, I don't think I've ever seen you so happy."

She gave Shawn a smile.

He glanced at Al. "You're the first person we're telling that Kayli and I are getting married."

Al laughed and walked over to Shawn and held his hand out. "Congratulations. You've got yourself a smart, brave woman." Then Al turned and gave Kayli a quick hug.

"Now let's get the tough stuff out of the way." Al was all business again. "I have to separate you for the interviews." He led Kayli into the first interview room and Shawn to the next. They lingered at the doors, gazing at each other, until Al came back with the detectives who would take their depositions.

~~~

Kayli finished first and went back to Al's office. They chatted until Shawn entered.

He held out his hand. "You ready to go get Michael?"

She jumped up. "Yes!"

Al chuckled and stood. "Congratulations again, and invite me to the wedding."

She'd never been to Jackie's house, but Shawn had gotten her address that morning and let her know they were coming. He told her not to tell Michael, so he wouldn't expect them every minute all day. It was late afternoon before they arrived.

They got out of the car to the sound of children's voices in the backyard. Kayli raced to the chain link fence. "Michael!"

His head turned, and he jumped out of the sandbox. "Mommy!" His little legs pumped and his arms swung, taking him to the fence. He'd grown in the time they were apart, time she'd never get back. There'd be more heartbreaking changes, too, she was sure. New things he'd learned to do, using new words.

Jackie got up from a chair on the deck and let them in. Kayli scooped up her son and twirled as she hugged him. She lost her footing and Shawn steadied her.

Michael glanced at him. "You were on the computer with Mommy."

Shawn took Michael's hand in a formal shake. "I'm Shawn. It's nice to meet you."

Kayli's heart swelled. Shawn, Michael and she were a new family. Tears pricked her eyes and she couldn't hold them back.

Michael put his hands on her cheeks. "Mommy, are you sad?"

"No. I'm really, really happy. I missed you so much. And it's not just you and me anymore. Now we have Shawn."

Michael tipped his head. "Like Kim has Donny for a dad, and Dom has Ethan for a dad?"

Surprise lit Shawn's face, followed by a softening. He

181

already cared.

"I'd like for us to be friends."

Michael tipped his head, and squinted. "Okay."

Shawn smiled. He wrapped his arms around the two of them.

Jackie put her hand on Kayli's shoulder. "Now your family is complete."

Shawn stared into Kayli's eyes. "Not yet, but give us time."

She liked the sound of that.

Epilogue

Fourteen months later, Shawn strode down the hospital corridor with Michael's hand in his. Michael looked up at him, "Dad, are we almost there? I want to see Delaney."

"It's just around the corner, son."

They stepped into Kayli's room and Michael yelled, "Mommy," as he ran to her. She helped him climb up onto the bed.

Shawn paused in the doorway, blinking back tears. His family. He hadn't known he could feel so much love for anyone. His heart swelled with love for these three people. Kayli held her hand out to him and he hurried to the far side of the bed. He took his wife's hand, kissed her soft lips, then leaned down and dropped a gentle kiss onto his daughter's forehead.

Kayli pulled her hand from Shawn's and unwrapped the baby. "Michael, you have to talk quietly. Delaney is sleeping." Kayli lifted up a little hand and Michael touched it.

"She's so little," he whispered. He looked up at Kayli. "Is Kim's sister going to be this little, too?"

Kayli laughed. "Yes, but she's not going to be born for two more months. By then, Delaney's going to be bigger."

The baby opened her eyes.

"Delaney's awake!" Michael said.

Shawn touched his son's shoulder. "You talk to Delaney, Michael. I want to talk to your mom."

Michael leaned close and started whispering to his sister.

Kayli raised her eyebrows. He smiled and pulled a small

box out of his pocket. Since their daughter was in one of Kayli's arms, he opened it for her. She gasped. "Oh, Shawn." She touched the necklace. Her eyes filled with tears.

"I took it about a month ago. I hoped you hadn't noticed and thought you lost it. I had the jeweler add another circle of diamonds around the first circle for our love. Then he added a small gold circle beside Michael's for Delaney."

"It's beautiful, Shawn. Thank you." She pulled him down for a kiss. "Can you help me put it on?"

He removed the necklace from the box and connected it behind her neck. She touched it, then caressed Shawn's cheek. He leaned down and kissed her.

"Mommy, your necklace got bigger," Michael said.

Kayli laughed. "Yes, your dad did it. Do you remember what it means?"

Michael touched the inner diamond circle. "That circle is you and my first daddy. This one is me. Is this one Delaney?" He touched the new gold circle.

"Yes. And the bigger outside circle is for the love your second dad and I have for all of us."

"Can we go home now?" Michael asked. "I want to show Delaney to Kim."

"Very soon." Kayli chuckled.

Shawn ruffled his son's hair. "Michael thinks it's the best thing we ever did to move to a house two doors down from Kim."

The End

If you loved the stalker part of this story, then you may enjoy, *Summer Love*.

Someone's trying to kill her, and there's only one man she wants to keep her safe.

Summer can't help the way her heart pounds whenever she's near Noah. But she should be spending time with the father she just found, not his stepson.

Noah's life is exactly the way he wants it. Then she shows up. Because all his relationships have ended badly, he tries to ignore his attraction to Summer. However, it's not long before he can't stay away from her.

But the man trying to kill Summer's mother may have switched targets. And Noah will do anything to keep the woman he's fallen for safe.

Available on Amazon
https://www.amazon.com/dp/B09Z2378M7

Thanks for reading. I hope you enjoyed my story. I would love if you left a review of my book on your favorite Book sites. Thank you.

Books by Deborah Wallace

Wounded Warrior Hearts Series (Clean Romance)
Wounded Warrior Hearts: Steven
Wounded Warrior Hearts: Amy
Wounded Warrior Hearts: Russ

Rawlins Series (Paranormal Romance – Witches)
Kathleen's Legacy
Jason's Forbidden Woman
Jamie's Trials
Adam's Redemption
Kristy's Puzzle
Tony's to Protect – *Fall 2022*

Choice Series (Romantic Suspense)
Second Choice
Third Choice
No Choice
Her Choice
Series complete

Unknown Series (Romantic Suspense)
Father Unknown
Killer Unknown – *Summer 2022*

Other Books (Romantic Suspense)
I Shot the Sheriff
New Memories
Your Love Belongs to Me
Summer Love

Check out my website for details on these books and where to find them. You can also sign up to receive emails when I have a new book. www.DeborahWallaceBooks.com.

You can find my books on my Amazon author page. amazon.com/author/deborahwallacebooks

About Deborah Wallace

Someone suggested I try writing, and stories started populating my brain, begging to be put on paper (or my computer screen).

I've got quite a number of books under my belt, but the ones I keep coming back to are the romantic suspense. When I wrote the first *Rawlins* book, I thought it would be the only paranormal. Then I said 'what if…' and now children of the first characters and a couple of friends have books.

I have been called a Jane-of-all-trades, from seamstress to house and furniture designer/builder to computer programmer to technical writer and bookkeeper. I even do car maintenance. I've also guided a team of 'Future Problem Solvers'.

I grew up in Michigan, but Massachusetts has been my home for more years than I care to think about. I love the history here, the museums and antique houses, the seacoast and hiking trails.

My three children have grown and scattered, but my husband is by my side, encouraging my writing.